STALKED

"IF I CAN'T HAVE YOU, NO ONE CAN"

Ebonie McBrayer

with Jocelyn Estes

ISBN 978-1-953223-49-4 (paperback)
ISBN 978-1-953223-48-7 (digital)

Rushmore Press LLC
1 800 460 9188
www.rushmorepress.com

Printed in the United States of America

Contents

CHAPTER 1

How It All Started

Amanda, spring break, 2014

This bitch Kerry, also known as KK, is fucking with the right one. My heart doesn't even beat the same anymore. A part of me will always feel broken, and I will always feel separated from the world.

Everything was okay until spring break. This is how my life went from being happy to me wanting to kill that bitch.

It all started when high school let out for spring break. We would be graduating in May. Some of us would be starting college in the summer to get ahead, while others would sit out until August. We decided to party together before we went our separate ways.

The hotel was packed with high school and college students.

In the lobby, there was nowhere to sit. The leather couches and chairs were already taken. Some people were sitting on the arms of the couches, while others sat on their luggage. They were all on their phones checking Facebook, talking among themselves, or taking selfies while they waited to register as guests. I don't know how everyone ended up here, but it was a five-star hotel. Who wouldn't want to stay somewhere nice on an occasion like this? We already had reservations, so there was no changing hotels. Besides, if we did, we probably wouldn't find another good one. I'm sure they were all packed, including the cheap, rundown ones.

We all made our number-one goal senior year to go to Myrtle Beach in North Carolina. We were all so excited, as this would be our first time on vacation without our parents.

We all planned for the trip this past year, so we took part-time jobs and asked our parents for allowances, so we'd have money to blow. Michelle's parents paid for the rental car and two rooms—one for Michelle and Kerry to share and one for me and my twin, Allen. Our rooms were side by side. We all stayed in one room until we got sleepy.

When I woke up that next morning, I checked my phone and saw I had no missed calls. I guessed Kerry and Michelle were still sleeping. *Allen likes to sleep in a little late,* I thought.

I got out of bed, slid my bunny rabbit slippers on, and opened the curtains. The sun was shining brightly, and I could see the ocean. It was breathtaking. Looking down from the fifth floor, it seemed as if there were a few hundred people already on the beach. I lifted the curtains and walked toward the balcony. I opened the sliding door and walked out to a breeze.

The weather was astonishing. I couldn't believe how wonderful it felt. There wasn't a cloud in the sky.

I ordered us room service for breakfast. It was covered with the cost of the room and kept us from getting in the car and searching for a place to eat. The hotel was not too far from the beach so we all could walk.

Ring. Ring. Ring.

I ran back inside to check my phone. Michelle was calling.

"Hello," I said.

"Hey, girl."

"Hey, I'm glad you up. The beach looks so beautiful."

"You already been down there?"

"No. I was just looking at it from my balcony."

"Oh," she said. "Well, have you eaten yet?"

"Yeah."

"Okay. Then come down to the first floor. By the way, Allen is still asleep."

"Kerry is too," she said. We both already knew that was due to them staying up late the night before.

"All right, let me throw on some clothes," I said as I walked over to my luggage to pull out a shirt and a pair of shorts.

Michelle and I were excited about the stay and ready to get the day started. We were up way too early, so that meant we got ready too soon.

While sitting around waiting, we decided to go lounge around in the hotel lobby.

Killing time and meeting new people, we noticed we were not the only ones waiting on our friends to get up and head to the beach. We could hear the conversations from some of the other people here.

Two guys walked over to us and introduced themselves.

"Hello, beautiful. What's your name?" one said.

"Amanda. And this my friend, Michelle, who I call Elle," I said.

"Hello, Elle. I'm Cory and this is my cousin Tony. Are ya'll from around here or just visiting for spring break?"

"Spring break," said Michelle. "What about you guys?"

"I stay here," Cory said. He pointed at Tony and said, "He comes here twice a year for spring break and summer. Would you all like to join us on my dad's yacht, it'll be here this coming Saturday? It's better than just sitting on the beach."

"That's if ya'll didn't have anything else planned for today," said Tony as he kept his eyes on Michelle.

I could hear his southern slang breaking through. He was a handsome guy, with silky, glossy, curly hair and peanut butter–complexed skin. He was tall and slim, but I could see the definition in his masculine body.

His cousin Cory, on the other hand, was banging with muscles. His body was thicker and masculine, and he had a low fade with a thin goatee. He had a darker tint to his skin. Both were very handsome and well mannered. I could tell someone was raising them to be gentlemen.

"Well, right now, we're just waiting on my brother and friend to wake up so we can go to the beach," I said.

"Oh, so you're not here with your boyfriend?" Cory asked.

"No, I don't have one," I replied. "What about you?"

"No, I do not have or care to have a boyfriend."

We both giggled, then I said, "My bad," with another light giggle. "Not the way I wanted that to come out." I said under my breath, "Do you have a girlfriend?"

"Nawl, but I would like to get to know you if you don't mind."

I gave Cory my number, and we just stood there making conversation. Michelle was talking to his cousin, so we just chilled in the lobby getting to know them. They seemed like good guys—not too flashy or full of themselves. Besides, they both dressed and smelled nice. Their parents must have been wealthy.

"What do you think you are doing, Amanda?" Allen asked in a mad voice. "We didn't come here so you could meet boyfriends." He gave them a mean glare.

"That is not what this is about," Cory said as he stood up to shake Allen's hand.

"Get that shit out my way, homeboy. This my twin sister, and she is too young to be talking to some college jock!"

"Whoa! Now come on. I wasn't trying to get at your sister. I was just killing time before going to the beach with my friends. My dad owns a yacht, and we were just inviting some people who looked cool to add to the party list. You guys are invited to join us if you want."

"I think we can manage our own fun this week. Thank you," Allen replied in a sarcastic tone.

I stood up and said, "No. You can manage your own fun, but Elle and I are going on a party yacht with Cory and his cousin Tony. You are not Dad. I can handle myself."

Cory responded, "You guys, it really is cool if you want to come. We will not be in your way." He looked over at Kerry and winked. "It's just we'd rather you not drink if you are underage. The bartender will be checking for ID."

Looking over at Kerry, she gave a nod, and we all agreed to have fun on the party yacht. I saw Cory give her a smile and another wink, but I paid it no mind.

"Meet us here Saturday at three, and we can head over to Myrtle Beach together. I promise we are going to have the best time of our life."

~

Saturday afternoon, we all met up and headed out to the beach.

Pulling up, we noticed a lot of people were setting up spots for their lounge chairs and playing volleyball. Some were on Jet Skis or water skis.

We all started to load up on the yacht to sail and party. It was beautiful—all white with leather seats that were peanut butter brown. It had a pool and seashell-shaped lounge chairs. It was like being on the beach but without the sand.

Downstairs was a bedroom with a king-size bed and a sixty-inch TV on the wall. Its bathroom was the size of my bedroom. It had an open shower and a hot tub next to it.

The bar had a bartender, and next to it was a kitchen with a chef—just like Cory said. This was something I might see in a movie. To be on one was amazing! Who would have thought in a million years we would be on a yacht?

I was nervous and a little afraid of all the water that surrounded us. Michelle knew how I was feeling, so she came and calmed me down a bit. Her parents were rich, so she was used to events like this.

Once the yacht started sailing away from the shore, it all felt like a dream come true. The water was even more beautiful out here. It was aqua blue. I had never been on a boat this big. It had loud music, people drinking and talking loudly, and no adults to block the fun.

"Hey, beautiful want to play poker with us?"

I looked beside me to see Cory. I smiled and invited myself to the seat in front of me. We played a couple of rounds until one of the guys said, "Lets light this party up. How about a game of twenty-one? Loser has to strip, but to keep it clean, no one gets naked."

We agreed to the terms of the game, and it was on. I was the best at playing twenty-one, so I had no worries that any clothes would be leaving my body—even though I was not shy about my body.

At five feet five and 146 pounds, with perky breasts, I was a real catch. None could compare to my almond brown complexion and my curvy hips. It was no wonder Cory wanted to see. I do not blame him. But I couldn't help but realize he had his eyes on Michelle, who, by the way, was every bit my competition. She was busy laughing and having fun with Tony, so she didn't see him eyeballing her.

She had a nice light tone; long, curly black hair flowing down her back; gray eyes; and a killer smile. She was beautiful. Standing shorter than myself, she was about five feet four with breasts the size of grapefruits, full and soft. She had sexy abs and a nice butt, but not as round as mine. I have to say, I did have that advantage over her. But overall, she was kindhearted. I can see why Tony was all over her.

What I didn't like was how Cory's eyes were glued to Kerry now. She was standing with my twin brother, smiling at the conversation they were having.

She stood the same height as me, five feet five, and weighed 138 pounds. She was light like Michelle but not as bright. She had comfortable-sized breast, washboard abs, and a round butt for a light-skinned girl. Now, you see, I wanted Cory for myself. I thought he was into me since I had given him my number.

But the way I kept catching him look at Kerry had me thinking otherwise. I hoped Allen hadn't scared him. He did make me feel like I was a little girl. But that was his way of protecting me, being he was my twin brother.

I'd had a thing for Cory ever since I saw him checking into the hotel early this week. I never said anything to anyone. We had only one more day to have fun, and I was overjoyed that we had the chance to do so together.

Wanting to show off my body to get his attention back on me, I started losing on purpose just to get his eyes back on this side of the table. As I removed my T-shirt, it worked like a charm.

"Damn, baby. You're so sexy!" He said as he came closer to me. He whispered in my ear, "This game is finished. I don't want no one else to see my soon-to-be girlfriend all half-naked. Let's go up top to talk and stick our feet in the pool."

Mission accomplished, I said to myself. We headed up top for some fresh air and a better view. Once we left, everyone started to do their own thing. As we were getting alone and the party was going well, I could see from the area I was sitting that Allen and Kerry were getting a little closer to each other. I paid it no mind; I was having my own fun. Michelle and Tony played pool ball inside the pool. I saw him grinding all up on her and swimming all around her. That made me want to get inside the pool as well.

"Let's get in the water and have fun like those two," I suggested.

He agreed. As we lowered our bodies into the pool, I could feel him gripping my waist, pulling me closer to him. I felt how strong his muscular body was.

"So, what are you into?" I asked.

"I play football for my college team. I also like to work out and build computers. My parents have big plans for me, and would much rather I go to college for computer technology than waste my time playing sports."

"Oh yeah? What college are you attending so I can apply as well?" I said, but I was only joking—until he said I should consider going to school in Texas with him. I thought once I cleared my head from this trip, I'd consider looking into it.

We both had the most amazing time on the yacht. Hell, we spent all our time together.

Late that Saturday night, while we were together in his room, I felt a connection like never in all my days of living. We talked and slow-danced to the music, Cory turning me around so he could dance behind me. He whispered in my ear, "I want you, and not just tonight but forever," breathing heavy with every word he said. I wanted him to. I knew I would never get a chance to see him again, so I just went with the flow.

He kissed me from my ear to my neck and down my back as he unzipped my dress. He gently placed his hand over my navel and turned me around. Face to face, we kissed.

As I could feel my body doing things, I never knew it could do, I wanted more.

"You are so soft and beautiful. I want you forever," he said as he laid me onto the bed. Pulling down my panties, he kissed my inner thigh. I let out a soft moan as he reached for the straps to my bra. I unhooked it from the front. Placing his lips on mine, he whispered, "Beautiful." As he kissed me deeply, I felt a funny but smooth sensation all over me. His lips traveled down my body. I moaned as he kissed me in places I never thought I could be kissed. I was on fire. He asked me if I was ready, and I told him yes.

That night I became a woman, and no one knew but Cory and me.

Leaving Cory's room, I quietly entered the room I shared with my twin. He was asleep but not alone. I saw Kerry's face laying on his chest, and neither had clothes on. Leaving the room in disbelief, I stood in the hallway pondering if I should just go back to Cory or knock on Michelle's door. Understanding that that was my brother's business, I just knocked on Michelle's room door. Half-asleep, she cracked the door, opening it all the way when she noticed it was me.

"Hey, can I bunk with you tonight?"

She pointed to the empty bed, which Kerry was supposed to be in. I lay down to get some rest, but all I could think of was Cory and all the fun we had.

I was in love, and I felt good about it.

～

The next morning, we all headed out for brunch and to say our goodbyes. I wrote down Cory's address and number so if I wanted to visit on my own I could. Stating that he was wealthy enough to send for me. He told me to consider the college he was attending.

We headed out to the mall for some last-minute shopping and dinner. I invited both Tony and Cory with us so he could see me off as we headed out.

"Hey, let's hit the beach one more time to see the waves and to have one last view of the sunset over the water," Michelle requested.

We all agreed and headed over to the beach for one last view. We took photos for memories, posing and having fun. Cory put his arms around Kerry and me in one photo. Tony and Michelle were on the right of us, while my twin stood next to me. The girl we asked to take the photo was very nice, and she allowed us to try out different poses. With the ocean view behind us, I knew this was a trip I knew I would never forget.

We talked and walked along the shore until the sun got lost behind the water.

Loading ourselves up inside the SUV, I made sure no one saw me kiss Cory. It felt as if we were losing each other forever. I was in love, and I was not ready to let it go.

As we drove off, we all set a time for us to drive, and we made a deal: whoever rode shotgun had to stay up with the driver. We stopped for snacks, gassed up, and headed out. We all talked about how much fun we'd had. All I could think about was that night with Cory. I fluffed my pillow and gazed at the moon until I fell asleep.

~

Opening my eyes, all I could see were bright lights in my face. I was being rolled into a room. I had no idea where I was or how I ended up here. I gathered my thoughts and remembered we were on the road. I had a terrible pain in my left arm and all over my body. All I could ask for was my brother.

No one said anything to answer my question. Frustrated, I asked again in a louder tone, and the nurse told me that I was in shock and needed to rest.

When I woke up again, my mother, father, and brothers were all standing over me. I must have been asleep for hours for them to be there with me.

Looking around the room for Allen, I asked, "Where is my brother?" The room grew silent, and my mother walked closer, placing her hand on my hair. She told me we had lost him. I couldn't believe any of the words she was saying. She said he had fallen asleep while driving. The room started spinning, and I became hysterical. I had lost my brother, my twin, the number one to my number two. He was gone. I needed someone to blame, and I had no other choice than to blame Kerry. She was supposed to be up with him while she rode shotgun. Why didn't she wake me up? We made a deal. Why didn't she wake me up?

As Michelle entered the room in a wheelchair later that day, I was afraid she was paralyzed until she stood up to hug me. With her hand wrapped up, she leaned over and put her forehead on mine, and we cried together. A few minutes later, Kerry entered the room with puffy red eyes and guilt on her face. Her head was wrapped in gauze, and it looked as if she were still bleeding from the blood stain on the bandage. I didn't care how she was doing. I wished she had died instead of my twin brother.

"You. It was you who killed my brother. You did this. Get out. Stay away from me!" I said as I tried to sit up in the bed.

"Baby, calm down," my dad said as he rushed over to me, trying to keep me from sitting up.

My brother walked over to Kerry and rolled her out of the room to keep me from getting even madder than I already was. I overheard him say, "Just stay away from her for a while. She is hurt and can only see her side of things. She will forgive you later. We do not blame you for Allen falling asleep. She just needs someone to blame, as always. She will come around."

Michelle didn't know what to do. I could tell she was concerned about Kerry, but being the good friend, she was to me, she stayed by my side. Mad as hell at her, I gave her a smirk once she noticed Michelle staying by my side and not running up behind her. Hurt by the careless behavior of my so-called friend, I was furious.

~

Finishing up school and preparing for graduation and college, I wanted to start the next chapter of my life with a clean slate. I paid Kerry a visit to clear the air and forgive her for falling asleep on my brother while he was driving. I knocked on her door and stood there for ten minutes to see if she would open it. She never came to the door, so I knocked once more. Then I saw a UPS truck pull into the driveway. I walked to the side of the porch where no one could see me. She opened the door before he had the chance to knock a second time.

"Hi, I have a package for Kerry Fitzpatrick."

"Yes, that's me," she said as she signed for her package. Now, I know she had heard me knock if she heard him. She is fucking something else. I don't know what my twin brother saw in her.

"Is there anything else?" she asked as he gawked at her.

"No, no, ma'am. That will be all ..." he said, as if he had more to say. I just kept my cool until he walked off. He sat in his truck for a split second, then returned to her door and knocked. He was into her, he said, and asked for her number. He was not a bad-looking dude, so I went home and placed an order for a delivery so he could come by my house.

If she didn't want to open the door for me, then she was going to be my enemy for life. So, starting with this guy, I decided I was going to ruin her relationships before they even started.

How dare Kerry not open her door for me! Hell, she should have been apologizing to me for falling asleep. So, since she wanted to play hardball, I would show her how to play.

Later that week, the same deliveryman made a stop at my house to deliver items for my college dorm room. I took my packages and bent over so he could see how sexy my ass was in my little shorts as I placed them on the steps. He was watching and caught off guard. He cleared his throat as I signed for my package. He asked whether I had a boyfriend. I told him no, but he could be it if he played his cards right.

I knew he was an easy catch once I saw how easy it was to get his number. I followed them around a lot when they went on dates. I even saw their first kiss. I was going to ruin her if it was the last thing I did before I was off to college.

She was going to pay for how snobby she had been acting. She was no better than me, and I was going to bring her wannabe-perfect ass back down to earth.

Just wait and see what I have in store for Ms. Kerry.

CHAPTER 2

Girls Trip

Michelle, summer of 2017

It was a rainy Thursday morning, and it had already been pouring down in the wee hours of the night. The forecast called for a sunny afternoon, which I was thankful for, since I had just finished coloring my hair on Wednesday night.

These beautiful curls in my wet-and-wavy style could survive anything. Rain, sleet, hail, and snow, I thought as I shook my head to let the curls flow.

The two-tone colors of black and brown, streaked with blond, set off on my light-toned skin and brown-gray eyes. As I applied my natural-tone makeup, I could see it no other way.

"I love me," I said to myself as I was looking in the mirror. I was full of confidence and self-love. No one could have told me differently.

You know me, the girl who always must plan everything. I thought everything through. Every little detail mattered. I was picky about many things, so I even did my hair and makeup myself, as my mother had taught me. My girls and I would always sit in on her hands-on makeup training classes. She would also host makeup parties for her cosmetics line, Dreams Cosmetics.

I was just like her in most of my ways. I had to have everything in a certain way, form, and fashion. It can be very tedious and color coded, if I may say so myself. It's always a must that I be neat, clean, and on point.

It fit the bill of my dreams. I wanted to be a celebrity stylist. So that is what I went to school for. I made people look good. Some didn't need much, while others needed a miracle. No matter what, I was your girl for the job. Working my way up the ladder, I was about to graduate with two separate degrees and was ready for the real world.

Finishing my last touches on my work outfit, I thought to myself, *Well, I guess I'll get my truck serviced before we hit the road.* I kissed at the mirror, happy that I got to take my girl out for her birthday this weekend. For some reason, I seemed to be acting more like my dad these days, living life in the moment and celebrating my soon-to-be-completed accomplishments. Doing last-minute planning, kind of like I was doing now. I was pleased with my look, to say the least. I had given my look a more natural tone and a different approach due to the new colors.

I was a makeup consultant for my mother's cosmetics line. I was also approaching graduation for my business degree as well as my cosmetologist license. I was on a roll and ready to show her a good time. I had the money, so the trip was all on me.

I lost my parents in a flight crash on their way home from their twenty-sixth anniversary. It was the end of my senior year of high school and seven months after Allen's death. I was an only child and already knew the business. It was the hardest time of my life, but I pressed through. This made me wealthy at an early age. I still honored my parents' wishes by continuing to pursue my own dreams. I love and miss them, so I'm doing right by them in life. I know they would be proud of me.

I took out my phone to call my best friend, KK, also known as Kerry, who works for the dealership where I get my car serviced and detailed, inside and out. I never knew why she picked this job for herself. With that degree she has in accounting, you would think she'd be someone's financial advisor or something. She was always good with numbers and knowledgeable in math. Anyway, she was my best friend, as close to family as I had. She and her mother made sure I wasn't alone. She would allow Kerry to come over and stay the night with me so I wouldn't be in the house by myself.

"Hey, girl, you think you can squeeze me in today for a service and detail before the weekend?" I asked.

She blew heavily into the receiver. "Girl, nobody has time for your last-minute requests!" she responded in her less-than-professional manner of speaking she uses whenever her coworkers are not around.

I have a bad habit of waiting until the last minute when it comes to small matters, even when they are important to plan. I know I was pushing it by asking her to break the rules in front of her coworkers.

"So unprofessional. Just unacceptable!" I yelled playfully.

"I'm sorry, ma'am, but we are booked for the week. You will have to check back on Friday," she responded in a serious tone. I must admit, I didn't think she would get mad.

"Um, today is Friday. Are you going to squeeze me in, or do I need to cancel our surprise all-expenses-paid getaway plans for the birthday girl?" I said, ending the joke we had going. By the way, she didn't know I had already asked Drake if she could come.

Kerry responded, "Look, if you want me to break some rules, first you have to come correct or nothing will go right for either one of us. Nobody schedules appointments here but *moi*, okay?" she said in a ghetto tone.

We both burst into laughter.

Kerry cleared her throat and said, "I have you down for five this evening, so please be on time," she said in a professional tone so her coworkers would think she was talking to a regular customer. I was guessing someone had reentered the room, as she had gotten serious in a hurry. I didn't want her to risk her job for my sake, so I went along with it, and we hung up.

In the meantime, I headed off to work. Dreading this half-rainy day, I was glad six hours passed by quickly. I prepared myself to leave work and drop my truck off for the service. I was on my way out to my truck when a gentleman stopped me to hand me one of his business cards. He was from New York. He went on to say something about being new to this state and wanting to build his clientele. He worked for a national security company. I think he said his name was Jeff. He went on to ask questions about the city, which slowed me down a bit. He wasn't a bad-looking guy, but I was in a rush.

"Are you or anyone you know looking to protect their privacy?" he asked.

"I do have a broken alarm system at my current residence," I replied. "I have to do something about that once I get back from this trip."

"Then you need to give me a call as soon as you're available," he said with a sweet smile.

"Thank you. I know. I'll use your service if the price is right."

"I'm sure we can work something out," he said as if this were still all business after that flirtatious smile, he just gave me.

"I also do businesses, so if you ever need assistance, or know anyone else who does, feel free to call me," he said as he held out his hand to shake mine. I returned the shake. I was on my way to walk off when he said, "By the way, what's fun to do around here? You know, some adult mingling?"

I didn't want to be rude, but I was in a hurry, so I told him I had somewhere to be, then stuffed the card in my bag and proceeded to my truck, not giving him so much as a second glance. But I was so calling him when I returned home so he could fix my system.

As I walked into the lobby to sign in, I noticed the lobby was full of customers.

Damn, I should have known better, I said to myself, slightly upset I had to wait with what little entertainment I had. It looked as if Kerry was off. I didn't see her around after I checked in. My cell battery was low, and the magazines on the table didn't strike my interest.

I walked into the waiting area, wishing I had brought a book to read. I sat beside a mother who was feeding her toddler. I started checking my emails and social media notifications. As I was pondering what outfit I was going to pack and all the things my girl and I are going to do out of town this weekend, I heard a familiar voice call my name.

"Hey, Elle! Let's go grab a bite to eat while you wait. It is going to be awhile, and I know this good hibachi grill just two blocks away."

I grabbed all my belongings, and we headed towards the door. "Thank you so much for thinking of me and not going home," I said to KK as we walked out of the dealership. "With all those people waiting, I would have been sitting there all evening."

"You're welcome, girl. It's the least I can do. I know the wait will be long, and dinner will be on me."

We pulled up to the restaurant and exited the car just in time to witness an accident. You could pretty much guess someone was hurt looking at the way the vehicles were damaged and hearing the noise of the impact. My instincts kicked in quickly, and I pulled out my cell phone to call for help for the two parties involved.

I had a sudden flashback to when our neighborhood friend Allen fell asleep at the wheel coming home from spring break. We had had the best week at Myrtle Beach. Coming back so late, we were excited about all the fun we'd had, but we lacked rest.

That was a tragic moment for all of us. On our way home, everyone was up and conversing with one another. We all volunteered to drive, but Mr. I Got This just had to be stubborn at the wrong time. His twin sister, Amanda, was on the trip with us, but she had fallen asleep while we were still hyped about the trip. I was in the back with Amanda on Facebook live, posting that we'd had a blast and were heading back home. Just after that, I fell asleep, and when I woke up, I was in the hospital, sore all over and with an injured hand. Amanda blames KK for it all because she was up front riding shotgun. We all promised that whoever rode up front would stay awake with the driver.

Being the guy Allen was, he definitely told her, "I got this. You can get some rest." He was just that type of guy and friend, so I am pretty sure it went something like that.

Leave it up to Amanda. She will hate Kerri forever. I love them both, but I can tell that Amanda is a bit jealous of Kerry. Believe me when I say I am not just taking up for Kerry. I have just seen some of the things Amanda has done to her.

Waiting on the emergency helpers to respond, I snapped out of my thoughts. It still brought tears to my eyes. Drying my tears so no one would see them, I made the report to the 911 operator. She wanted me to stay on the line until helped arrive. I slipped back into my thoughts about Allen. He wasn't one of the lucky ones who had made it out all right. I had a sprained wrist, KK had a gash in her forehead that left a permanent scar, and Amanda had a broken arm.

Gosh, it's crazy how you can lose your life behind the wheel of a vehicle or make it out without as much as a scratch. Amanda has blamed KK ever since, and she moved away soon as we finished high school. She had always said that the two used to flirt, but Allen was feeling KK a lot more than she knew. Amanda used to get mad when KK would play hard to get. But somehow, Allen and I knew it was a front. Amanda just didn't get KK. That's why she was so hard on her. Even though she did have her moments, we all still hung together tight as tied knots.

I think that is why she blamed her. Amanda called me before she went off to school to say she was going to apologize to Kerry, but she said Kerry never came to the door. That's when she called it off and just left matters the way they were. She didn't know her like we did, and that's what made her bitter.

We waited until help arrived, and we entered the building for a quick dinner. Everything smelled so good, I was ready to eat soon as I sat down at the grill. Looking over at Kerry, I could tell she had felt some type of way about the wreck we had just witnessed. She took a deep breath and said, "So much for that Japanese rice wine I was going to order." I noticed she had become emotional, so I sat next to her in silence, rubbing the top of her back.

As we ate our meal, no one said a word. I could tell it was bothering her, so I went with the flow. She was still in deep emotions. Yeah, she had taken it hard, with Allen being the first boy she had ever loved. She would try to hide her feelings from me, but I knew better. It was noticeable during high school.

She and Amanda had grown close when she said they could date. She would call Allen on three-way, and I would listen to KK and Amanda tease Allen.

Sometimes, I wish I could take it all back. I wish I had said, "I'll drive first." That way, I would have known I had all our lives in my hands. I would have pulled over at a rest stop the moment I felt tired.

My cell phone vibrated inside my handbag, snapping me back to reality. It was the dealership, telling me my truck was ready. I cheered and did a little dance, bragging about all the fun to come this weekend. This put a smile back on her face and lightened the mood.

I learned a long time ago just to allow her to grieve in her own way. Otherwise, she would clown me out and get loud with the yelling. That's how she relieved her pain and pressure.

After gathering our things, we headed back to the dealership. KK was still a little upset but not as emotional as before. This was because I had played her favorite songs and sung them out loud at her. I was hoping she would come out of that somber attitude. I paid it no mind, just gave her some space to think about it. I would have wanted her to do the same for me.

Later that evening, after packing, I planned on getting some rest. I had learned from our past mistakes, and I made it my personal mission to be wide awake for this trip.

I loaded up the truck and set the alarm for 1:30 a.m., as well as the coffee maker, to make sure we were road ready. I put the TV channel on Style, because I love fashion and glamour. Then I fell asleep.

Getting Ready for My Birthday Weekend

Kerry

As I walked up the sidewalk to put my key into the lock, I sat on the swing on my porch and cried. I still felt bad for those people in that car accident. So many memories passed through my mind. All I could do was think about spring break and that horrible image of Allen stuck in my head. You see, no one knows that I was the one who called for help.

Likewise, I was the last one he spoke to. He told me he'd had fun with me and that I was the love of his life. He told me to stay calm and that everything would be okay. But I knew that wasn't true. I called out for Amanda, but he told me not to. He didn't want her to panic. I grabbed his hand and held it in mine as tears ran down my face and my heart beat uncontrollably.

Blood was running down his face from where the shattered windshield had cut him. When we hit the wall, the motor came forward, crushing him. It was hard for him to catch his breath. He knew he was dying, so he was determined to get out what he had to say. I could barely hear what he was saying. I kept having to move my ear close to his mouth, but I knew what was about to happen. He was about to leave me forever. He told me he had always loved me ever since we kissed by that oak tree in his backyard. I was seven, and he had just turned eight. I had no idea he still remembered that.

Snapping out of my thoughts, I could tell Drake was cooking something good. Something told me to call and tell him I was eating out with Elle. He also had music blasting. I thought he had to work late. Shrugging my shoulders, I turned the key to walk inside.

I tried to lift my spirit before I walked inside the house. I swear, that man can tell when something is bothering me. I didn't want him to worry. I went into the house, threw my keys and purse on the couch, and peeked around the corner into the kitchen. There he was, standing five feet ten, with his shirt off. We lived in a three-bedroom house, and one room had been turned into a gym/man cave. Bae was built. He had a muscular butt, a six-pack, toned arms, legs, and thighs. He was perfectly made and perfect to me.

We met when he delivered me my new Chanel bag, with matching heels, back when I was staying with my mom fresh out of high school. I was nineteen and he was twenty. He had just started at UPS, driving the delivery truck, and had recently started volunteering at the fire station twice a month. Three years later, we were still together. I just hoped he would ask me to marry him before I turned twenty-five, which was in about three years. I told him, but he just said, when he's ready, I will know it.

I couldn't help but stare at him and the way he was tossing this salad, with his big, strong arms that made me want to drop to my knees. I started caressing my body and imagined us making love on the kitchen table. As soon as I opened my eyes, his chest was in my face, and I started breathing out of control.

He backed away from me to take a good look at me. He grabbed his penis and winked his eye. He knew what was on my mind without me having to say it.

"When we get finish eating, you can have your dick," Drake said, grabbing my hand and putting it in his pants so I could feel how hard it was. "But we going to eat first, and when we're finish, I'm going to eat you."

He grabbed my hand and led me to the table, pulling my chair out for me to sit down. Then he went to the other end to sit.

"Baby, this steak and salad are delicious. Thank you," I said as I lightly ate what he had prepared for me. I wasn't trying to be rude, but I was already full.

"You know I'm going to take care of you. The rest of your gifts are in the bedroom."

I couldn't do anything but smile.

"You are the best!" I said with excitement. "Oh, Elle wants to take me to Atlanta for my birthday, her treat, but if you have plans already in motion, then we can reschedule," I said, hoping he would say yes to this trip.

"Baby, I will be here when you get back. You never go anywhere or do anything. Go enjoy yourself with your friend."

"Yeah, you're right, and it's only for the weekend," I said, happy as hell that he didn't mind.

He reached in his pants pocket and handed me two thousand dollars.

Here. Go buy you a few outfits, something they aren't wearing out here.

"Thank you, baby!" I said as I jumped up grabbed the money. I started undressing, backing up towards the bedroom and motioning my finger for him to get up from the table and follow, just as I expected him to do.

"You want it, or do you need it?" Drake asked while he was undoing his pants.

"I need it … I need to feel you inside me," I said, climbing into the bed with my eyes glued on him.

He picked me up and scooted me off the edge into the middle of the bed, kissing my neck and playing in my juices with his finger.

"Damn, baby, you wet," Drake said, whispering in my ear.

"It's all yours, baby."

"It is, and it better be," Drake said, going down on me.

"Oh ... yes ..." was all I could say as I pulled his head deeper into me. He kept coming up for air and going right back down. After a few more minutes down there, he came up and went right into stroking. He flipped me over and slapped my ass, holding on to my waist in a doggy position.

"It's my turn," he said. Then he lay on his back with his hands behind his head. I crawled over and climb on top and started riding him like a bull. Bouncing up and down on his penis, I grabbed both of my breasts, squeezing my nipples until I couldn't take it anymore. Seeing me playing with myself turned him on even more, until he couldn't take it anymore and exploded inside me. After that, he couldn't move. He didn't want to move, so we just lay there and went to sleep. I wanted to make sure he missed me while I was away.

Ring ... ring ... ring ...

The sound of his phone going off.

Damn, who the fuck calling him?

He was sleeping like a baby. Hell, we both fell asleep. He rolled over to the nightstand to see who was calling and pressed the silent button.

"Baby, who was that?" I asked in a sleepy voice.

"That was Chris. He didn't want nothing. I'll call him back," Drake said, rolling over to hold me. We fell back asleep.

The alarm went off at midnight. I got out of bed and headed to the shower to freshen up. I wasn't worried about putting on any makeup or trying to look cute for anyone, because what I wanted was over there lying in the bed butt naked. Since I already knew what clothes and shoes I was taking, it didn't take long to pack. We going to be sitting for a while, so I threw on a white T-shirt, tights, and my Chuck Taylors, something comfortable but cute that showed off my curves.

Ring ... ring ... ring ...

I rushed over to my phone. It was on the floor under our clothes. I could barely hear it ring. It was Elle.

"Hello."

"Hey, you ready?"

"Hold on a second," I said, trying to connect my Bluetooth.

"Hello … hello … KK," Elle yelled in my ear.

"Girl, I said hold on. I was connecting my Bluetooth."

"Oh, well, I didn't hear you," Elle said.

"That's because I set the phone down while I was talking." We both started laughing at this mishap.

"So, are you ready?" Elle asked.

"Yeah. I'll be there in thirty minutes," I said as I continued dressing while on the phone.

"All right, cause I'm trying to be on the road by two. I have coffee as well."

"Bet. I'll be leaving in a second."

"Okay, bye," Elle said.

"Bye," I replied as we both hung up.

I grabbed my bags and placed them by the front door. I walked back into the bedroom to wake up bae to let him know I was about to leave.

"Bae, wake up," I said, kissing on him. "I'm about to leave," I said in a light voice.

"Grab my pants off the floor so I can watch you leave. I don't need you going outside this late by yourself," he replied.

I gave him his pants, and we walked to the door. He slid his shoes on, grabbed my bags, and headed to the truck with me.

"I am going to miss you," I said.

"And I'm going to miss you too, baby," he replied, walking over to kiss me. He shut the rear passenger door. "Call me as soon as you get there. Now, hurry off. I'm about to get back in the bed," he said, talking through his yawn.

"Okay, baby. I love you."

"Love you too, and don't forget to call," he said

"I won't."

He walked to the house, stood in front of the door, and waited for me to pull off. I drove for about a mile. Then I thought to call Elle to let her know I was on my way. As I reached in the passenger seat, I didn't feel it. So, I went through my purse, but I didn't see it there either.

"Damn," I said in a frustrated tone.

I turned around and headed back to the house. I pulled up into the driveway and went inside. I headed to the bedroom, and I could hear the shower running. I looked at the bed. Drake had clothes laid out. I hurried to the shower and slid the glass door open.

"Whoa ... Girl, you scared me."

"Where you are going?"

"Chris called back and asked if I wanted to get out for a little bit. So, we going to hit up Little Rock and probably stop by a bar. What's wrong, y'all not going?" he said, still washing his body.

"Yeah, we still going. I left my phone here. Why you just didn't tell him you were asleep."

"Bae chill out. By the time I lay down, he called. I told him no at first, but then I couldn't fall back to sleep. I called him back and said yes."

Ring ... ring ... ring ...

My phone sounded off in my hand.

"It's Elle. I gotta go."

Running out the door, I heard him yell, "Be careful."

"Hello."

"Where are you?"

"I'm on my way now. Give me ten minutes," I lied so I wouldn't hear her mouth off about being late.

I was kind of in my feeling. Suddenly, he is getting up and leaving. But he's always with Chris, so I wasn't tripping too badly.

I made it to Elle's house in fifteen minutes. She was already in her truck, waiting on me. I parked, grabbed my bags, and jumped in the truck with her.

"That was more than ten minutes," Elle said, handing me my cup of joe.

"I know. I left my phone at home and had to turn around and grab it. You know black folks never on time," I said jokingly.

"Anyway, what do you think about going to Dallas instead of Atlanta?"

I turned to see what Elle would say.

"It's whatever you want. It's your birthday weekend. I'm down as long as we get the hell outta Arkansas," she said.

"Let's ride then," I said as Elle pulled off. "I'll start searching for a hotel." I grabbed my phone and searched for five-star hotels in Dallas, Texas.

"Okay, girl, get a nice one and check the reviews. While you're at it, look in my wallet and grab my credit card. Find a good one and put it on reserve so we can already be booked."

First, I needed to find some music for our ride. I flipped through the stations, but nothing good was playing.

It's good, I thought, to grab a few CDs, like K. Michelle, Tamar Braxton, and Beyoncé. We listened to them and some of Elle's favorites—Usher, Tank, Kehlani, and Dvsn, some new group she heard on YouTube. The whole six and a half hours, we sang along and danced in our seats. We stopped once for gas and bought ourselves some snacks, then switched seats to even out the drive for this trip.

"We're here," I said, pulling into the parking deck of the Statler hotel.

"Good. Let's go in and get set up. I'm sleepy," Elle said.

We grabbed our bags and headed inside to the lobby. We went to the front desk to check in and grab our key.

"Good morning. Welcome to the Statler."

"Morning. I just made a reservation for Michelle Dream."

"Yes, ma'am. Let me just check you in. May I see your ID?"

"One second," Elle said. She placed her bags on the floor and took her ID out of her wallet to hand to the lady.

"Thank you," she said as she handed it back. "Two queen beds, nonsmoking, city view premium room. Take the elevator up to the eighteenth floor. Your room number is on the back of the card slip. Thank you for choosing our hotel. Please enjoy your stay. By the way, I love your makeup and skin-glow serum."

"Thank you. I'm glad you do. I will return in just a sec to give you some samples I keep with me to expand my clientele," Elle said. She ran out to the truck for her party sample bag. She gave her two, just in case she had a friend or family member who wanted to try out her products.

Once we got in the room, we were happy about how nice it was. Elegant and classy looking, something nice in case I wanted to bring Drake one day for a getaway, just the two of us.

Elle went to her bed, and I sat on mine. Speaking of Drake, I pulled out my phone so I could call him and let him know I'd made it. Looking over at the clock, it read 7:12 a.m.

"Who are you calling? Oh, never mind. It's Drake!" Elle teased.

"I told him I would call as soon as we made it, but he's not answering," I replied, not trying to look all sprung and in love and shit.

"He's probably asleep. I mean it is seven in the morning," Elle said, pulling the covers back to get into her bed.

"Well, he told me to call. That's why I'm calling him."

I was about to leave a message, but I told myself he would call once he saw he missed my call. Paying it no mind, I fell asleep.

When I opened my eyes, the sun was shining bright as hell in my face. Elle, that ol' playful ass girl, opened the curtains from one end to the other, filling the room with light.

"Wakey wakey," she said, giggling and dancing her way to my bed. All I could hear was her snapping her fingers, as if music was encouraging her to dance. I looked over at my cell phone to see if Drake had called.

"This boy has lost his damn mind!" I yelled. "Why hasn't he called me back? He seen my number on his phone. Hell, he keeps that thing attached to his fingers. So, I know he got my call."

I wasn't having this shit. I called him back to back to back, not giving a damn if I killed his battery. He waited good until I got out of town, and now not to answer? This was so not like him.

"Girl calm your nerves. We're here to have a good time. He'll call you back once you stop calling him back to back to back to back. His phone going to say 2:01, 2:02, 2:03, 2:04, and 2:05," Elle said, laughing.

"But you'd think he'd have enough sense to call and check on me. It's like he said, 'Fuck KK.'" I grabbed the pillow and hugged it. With my chin to my knees, I looked at the floor with worried thoughts in my head.

"Girl, he's probably calling but it's going straight to voicemail, or maybe he's asleep and can't hear it," Elle said as she turned away from the mirror to face my frustrated ass.

"Girl, why the fuck this boy isn't answering my phone? And it seems like it is ringing once and going to voicemail. I know he went out with Chris last night, so he may have a hangover," I said, defending my man.

"Look, I understand you mad—"

"How could you possibly understand how I feel. When is the last time you had a man?" I said with my head twisted, waiting for a response.

"You know what?" Elle said with her index finger up, waving it back and forth. "You didn't even have to go there. But I'm going to let that one slide since you're in your feelings. I'm about to shower and get dressed to go shopping and have some lunch. If you were smart, you would be doing the same."

Leaving the bedroom area and walking to the bathroom, she slammed the door behind her.

"If you were smart, you would be doing the same," I mumbled after her in a mocking manner with my face twisted up. "Fuck it," I said in a quiet voice as I sat up in bed and started texting his phone:

> Drake I know you see me calling you, this shit is really pissing me off. You need to call me ASAP.

CHAPTER 4

Oh No, She Didn't

Michelle

You mean to tell me I brought her ass all this way with me so she could hound him down? Like, what the fuck? She should have brought that nigga if she was going to flip out about him not answering, I said to myself in the shower.

I know I don't have a man in my life, but the point of this trip was for us to have fun. Let our hair down. We worked so hard for this, and now she all up his ass. Hell, I feel like this was a waste of money!

I continued to rub my body down with my wash, A Thousand Wishes, from Bath and Body Works. I was in an insolent-ass mood and was telling her off in my head. Looking in the mirror after my shower, I was mouthing off in silence about her unwanted behavior. Hell, she was killing my mood. So, I turned on my iPod and played my music. Putting on my makeup and moisturizing my body down, I could hear KK getting upset.

After taking a deep breath, I walked back into the room to grab some more of my stuff to finish getting ready.

Stuck in the same spot with little to nothing done, I already knew this trip was over before it even began. I walked back into the bathroom to put on my finishing touches, then back to the room.

"You want us to just go back home and try this trip another time?" I said.

She shook her head no, but I could feel she wanted to so bad. I picked her thoughts.

"What would make you happy right now? Because I don't want to be here if you do not want to be here."

She got up out of her seat and went into the bathroom, leaving me here with my own set of questions.

I grabbed a shot-sized wine bottle from the minibar fridge. Not knowing what to do next, I turned my music back on and put my earbuds in. Feeling pretty upset, I just chilled with my wine and music.

I was wearing a black off-the-shoulder drawstring crop-top and tight all-white Eddie Bauer capris, ripped at one knee. They hugged my hips and thighs tightly. I was ready just in case I had to go and have fun alone. I was game, standing in the mirror and admiring my body as I took a quick selfie.

I love KK, and I do want her happy. I didn't know things would take such a left turn. Was she worried about his safety, or did she suspect he was cheating? That was the question.

Getting crunk off my playlist, I was about to head to the mall. I wanted to be fresh when we went out tonight. *If* we went out. I might be going by myself.

She was in the bathroom for about an hour. Then she reappeared looking as beautiful as ever.

"Didn't expect me to jump clean on you really quick huh?" KK said in a ready-to-party kind of voice. She appeared in a burgundy off-the-shoulder Alleyoop jumpsuit from Lulu's that I always ask for when I go into her closet. It still had the tag on it the last time I saw it. Now this heffa was geed up to the T, if you know what I mean.

"I'm game for whatever, girl. You know me."

"Now, that's what I'm talking about, girl. Let's shine on 'em," I replied, happy that my best friend was happy and ready to kick it.

We left the hotel and drove straight to the mall. Shopping was my thing, and it was therapy for the both of us. Being that it was her birthday, her shopping was all on me, a way to get her mind off her man and on to some fun.

Now, please, do not get me wrong. I'm not one to hate. I care if he calls my girl back. But she needs to give him time to respond. Like, I know he loves her. Maybe he's just tied up with something important. He is a hardworking man, you know. But nobody wants to worry when they are miles and miles away. I hope he get it together and responds to her message. Don't need to have my friend out here worrying. No, sir.

CHAPTER 5

He Is All Mine

Amanda

Yeah, I knew better when I saw them two together. I was with him too; he was mine just as much as he was hers. I thought he said she was in Atlanta for her birthday weekend. Oh well, I was not going to stop my show for her. Hell, I was trying to get the man I really wanted by trying to make him jealous. I knew if Cory saw me here with him, he would become jealous and want me back.

I left the room to go get us something to eat. I had called Cory and asked if he could meet me at the pool on the top floor of the hotel where we were all staying. So, when I saw Kerry and Michelle, I wanted to say hi to Michelle, but I didn't give a damn about Kerry. Just like she didn't give a damn when she fell asleep on my twin brother. So, here and now, I still didn't give a damn if she was here.

I stood clear of the two of them walking out of the Statler Hotel. I had food in my hands, and I eased off to the side so they wouldn't notice me. But now that she was here and not in Atlanta, it wasn't on me if she found out.

I had been planning for this weekend for two months. I was planning for Cory to find me and my new man together, to make Cory jealous and show him what he had lost. I was going to have my fun with no interruptions.

I did miss my girl Michelle, but Kerry always stayed attached to her hip like a loyal little puppy. I always thought she hung around Michelle because she was rich from her mom and dad. But maybe there was some real loyalty in that bitch. I don't know, but I didn't like her. After she fell asleep on my brother, Kerry could kiss my ass. But enough about her. I was here with my man, and we was going to have fun this entire weekend. Like I said—with no interruptions.

Heading back to my room, I slid the key card inside the slot. The door opened.

"Hey, baby, I'm back, and I have something to eat."

"Damn, baby, what took you so long? I was getting worried."

"I had to wait in a long-ass line for us. It is still hot and fresh," I said in a sexy, enticing voice. "Eat up so we can get back to us. I don't get to see you much as I like, but now we have the time, so let's not waste it."

We finished our meal, made love, and had a shower. We watched some good movies, went to have drinks at the lounge, and headed back to our room. I was in heaven with this man. He made me happy all the time. I really wasn't feeling him at first, under the circumstances, but now, I felt I was in love. We had been together for three years now, and I had him just like Kerry had him.

We went up to the rooftop lounge and stuck our feet in the pool. It was so beautiful up there. There were tables with lights on them, not too bright but dim so it felt more romantic. We talked about everything and anything that came to mind. We related on so many levels and had a lot in common. He wowed me with his lovemaking. When I tell you it was mind-blowingly good, you must believe me! I crave him every time he's away.

We enjoyed each other's company, and having drinks topped it all off. I could tell it had kicked in, and he could tell also. He rubbed his hand through my hair while I closed my eyes to the good feeling of the breeze. He lifted my dress up, moved my thong to the side, and then stopped. I opened my eyes, like, *why stop?* He looked at me, licking his lips the same way LL Cool J did in his videos. Then Drake got in the pool. I remained sitting on the edge while he came in front of my legs, spreading them apart so he could stick his finger inside me, moving it in and out. The feeling was so good, I was pushing against his hand so he could go deeper. My head fell backward as I started moaning. When I opened my eyes, I saw Cory across from us, looking at me with disgust in his eyes.

I was happy that he had caught me red-handed, but I also felt ashamed. We had been together just a couple of weeks ago.

I was about to move Drake's hand, until he just walked off without making a scene. I was about to get up and run after him, but the feeling Drake gave me was so hypnotizing, I couldn't move. I knew I had asked him to come to make him jealous, but the vibes Drake was sending? Shit, I wasn't worried about Cory.

I suggested we head back to the room for some more lovemaking, being that we only had this weekend before he headed back home. I knew Kerry was here, but my lips were sealed. If she caught us, then I would have killed two birds with one stone. I did what I had to do for Cory to see me with another guy. The fact that he just left let me know he was going to be calling me sooner or later. He never left his business unfinished.

I stood up after I dried my feet off. We headed back to the room, flirting the whole way there. In the elevator, we kissed and rubbed all over one another as he lifted my dress again, caressing my honeypot. I moaned in pure pleasure. This man knew how to handle my body and how to make me scream. I lucked up when I chose him. Even though my intentions weren't real at first, they are starting to become so real, to the point where I wanted him all to myself. But hey, it would soon be my turn—once I finished hurting the people who had hurt me.

We got off the elevator and walked down the hall toward the room. Kissing all over my body, he pulled my dress over my head. Kissing my exposed breast and fondling my love hole, he made me feel like a woman in every way.

Kissing, touching, and moaning, he laid me all over that room. From the doorway to the floor to the bed, he handled my body like a king. As we entered the shower, I washed him off and softly stroked his manhood, then placed my warm mouth on his rod and enjoyed every bit of it.

I could tell he enjoyed it. His legs were shaking like they were about to give out. I didn't stop. I kept him weak as I mouthed off his love stick, making him reach for my head and whisper, "Yeah, baby, suck this dick." I did only what I was told, and he didn't last a second longer. He yelled, "Fuck" as he busted all over the shower wall. I smiled because my job was completed for the night. We finished showering and laid our drunk asses down. As I was falling asleep, I was thinking of ways to finish my ruthless destruction of that bitch I hated so much.

Just wait and see just, wait and see.

Looking over at Drake, I kissed him, and he kissed me. He grabbed to cuddle me, and he told me he loved me. I told him the same, and we fell asleep in each other's arms. He didn't know I had blocked every woman's name in his phone, so he wouldn't be hearing from them until after I was done with him. And from the looks of it, he was mine. I knew this would surely set Kerry's attitude in the right direction: mad. That bitch is going to wish she stayed in my good graces.

CHAPTER 6

Long Time No See

Michelle

As we were on our way out to have fun tonight, an evening of shopping and eating, I called around to see if I could book us a VIP table at one of the hottest spots in Dallas. If I was going to do it for my best friend, I was going to do it right. So, I went to take a shower and laid out all the names of the spots I looked up. Once I got out of the shower, I headed to my bed to chill and order the things we needed to make her birthday as fabulous as ever. While I was at it, I was going to be looking for a potential date. It had been a minute since I had fun with a guy, and I felt I was ready to date again.

So, tonight I was going to have my eyes open. Hopefully, I'd find me someone who was not from Arkansas. Not that there is anything wrong with the men there. I just wanted mine from out of town.

"So, all you are going to do this whole weekend is call and check up on him?" I asked KK.

She replied, "Elle, it's really not like him not to call. We always check in with each other, sometimes twice a day."

I stared at my friend, and as I looked, I could see that she was upset, so I left the subject alone. I decided not to worry about booking any VIP tables. Hell, that would be a waste of money. I went to the rooftop to enjoy some time alone. I didn't know how to feel. I ordered myself a cocktail and sat alone while I flipped through my Facebook newsfeed.

I knew I had to give her space, so that is what I did. I didn't want her upset, so I didn't bother her with my silly plans. For all I knew, we might be doing this until she was ready to go home.

As I ordered another round for myself, I jumped at the sound of a baritone voice behind me.

"It's on me."

"Oh no, you don't have to do that," I said as he hurried up and told the bartender that it all was on him.

"Why are you paying for my drinks and you don't even know me?" I asked.

"You are still beautiful three years later," he replied.

Now, I know I'm not crazy, and I felt like this was a joke. Could he read minds, or did God step-in right-on time?

"Do I know you?" I asked.

"I believe so. Don't I look familiar to you?"

"Not at all," I said as I looked into his brown eyes down to his full lips and over his caramel-colored skin. Then back up to his eyes. As we gazed at one another, he replied, "I'm Tony."

"Tony who?" I asked, feeling instant chemistry booming between the two of us.

"Tony from spring break of 2014, as I recall," he said as his voice got deeper.

I looked back at him from head to toe. He did look a little familiar. But before I could say it, he said, "I put on some muscle playing college football. When we met, I was new to the team and had just started working out."

"Yes ... it is you ... hi, how have you been doing?" I said as I stood to embrace him.

"Good to see you too, and you still look the same—body still sexy as ever, I see."

I blushed at the sound of his compliments, and we shared drinks and laughter. It felt so good to have some male company. I almost forgot what it felt like to be flirted with. He was better looking now than he was then. I mean, he was tall like six feet, and his body was built like a wide receiver's. You know, tall and muscular. His complexion was caramel, and his hair was deep, wavy curls, silky and jet black. He was handsome this time around. Not to be mean, but he was just too frail when we first met.

We must have been at the bar for about an hour before I realized I had left KK back in the room.

"So, how are all your friends from spring break doing? Do you guys keep in touch?" he asked, interrupting my thoughts.

"We had an accident on our way home. I jammed my hand. Kerry has a scar on her forehead. Amanda broke her arm. Allen didn't make it," I said as tears filled my eyes.

"I'm so sorry to hear that," Tony said in a calm voice as if he was sad too.

"It's not your fault. You didn't know," I replied. "Kerry is two floors down. Tomorrow is her birthday. I brought her here to celebrate."

"You two should make reservations at this popular nightclub tonight," he said. I guessed it was an invitation.

"I wasn't going to go all out, but hey, who knows? It couldn't hurt to try something new somewhere else."

I corresponded to put the plans back in motions. I didn't want to put KK's business out there like that to Tony, so I told him that I would consider it.

"Speaking of KK, I need to go check on her. This was fun, Tony. We must do it again."

"Indeed, we must!" he said as he stood to pull out my chair and embrace me with another one of his strong hugs.

Smiling, I pulled back as I got a good whiff of his cologne. Man, he smells good. He handed me one of his business cards, and we departed for the evening.

Heading back to the room, I walked in and sat on my bed, smiling at the card I held in my hand.

"Where have you been? And who has placed a smile so big on your face? I want to know everything," KK said as she sat up to face my direction.

"I ran into Tony at the bar. Well, at first, I didn't notice it was him, but he seems to have remembered me," I said, still smiling.

"Tony who?" KK wondered.

"Spring break—tall, frail guy."

"Oh, I thought you said he was too scrawny for you back when we were in high school?"

"You should see him now, girl. He is stacked and very well groomed," I said, posing to indicate the muscles on his arms and chest. "We can conversate about the moment we spent talking when I come out of the restroom."

I went to the bathroom to freshen up and to let my excitement out in private. I was in a good mood and in need of that company from Tony. I was feeling myself now, smiling all in the mirror. I was happy about this trip, and no one or nothing could knock this big-ass smile off my face. Reminiscing over the smell and smile on this man, I was in awe of what I wanted to do next.

"Slow your roll, Michelle," I said to myself.

I didn't want to get overjoyed about a man I still don't know.

But the way I felt, I was open to get to know him more. We will see who Mr. Tony Brown is. But first, let me book this VIP table at this club here Tony talked about.

CHAPTER 7

What a Birthday!

Kerry

This weekend isn't going good at all. My girl mad at me and left me in this room alone. My man won't pick up the phone, and I'm scared something might have happened to him. I don't know what to think. But I'm sure if something happened, someone would have called and said something.

I heard the door unlock, and Elle walked in with a smile on her face. I was shocked, 'cause I expected her to be mad and have a bitch-don't-talk-to-me look on her face. But instead, she walked right by me all calm and sat on her bed.

"No, ma'am, I don't think so," I said with my hands on my hips.

"What?"

"How you come in smiling and go in the bathroom and come out still cheesing. What's got you all jolly?"

"Girl ... you wouldn't believe me if I told you."

"Stop playing and tell me."

"Remember Tony from spring break, on the yacht?"

"Tony ... Tony ..." I said, like saying his name twice would help me remember. "No, that name doesn't sound familiar."

"Yes, you do. Remember the two guys we got on the yacht with? One was talking to Amanda, and the other was trying to talk to me."

"Oh yeah, what about him?"

"Well," she said as she came over to my bed, smiling like she hit the jackpot, "I was on the rooftop getting a drink, and Tony pays for my drink. Then he tells me that after all this time, I still look good to him. At first, I didn't recognize him because he didn't look the same."

"For real? So how he looked?"

"Oh my God, he is so fine. You know, he was a little skinny ol' thing when we met him, but now he got muscles, and he's six feet, with sexy curls."

"I knew it had to be a guy, because you just don't come in smiling for nothing. What is he doing anyway?"

"He went to college here and decided to stay. Isn't that crazy? I never would have thought in a million years I would run into him again. Now either he's good with faces or I haven't changed much, because he remembered what I look like."

"Wow, but you know he was feeling you, and some people are just good with faces," KK said.

Elle got up to take a shower while I remained sitting in the bed, lost in my thoughts. I really do love Drake, and we been through a lot with one another. We done had our ups and down. He's not perfect, and he's done things I don't like. But I have forgiven him because I believe in us, and I'm not about to throw away our two-year relationship. Last year, on my birthday, we were supposed to go out, but he didn't come home, and I spent my birthday alone, calling him all night. He gave me some dumb-ass excuse, but I didn't believe him, so I packed my bags and moved out. This is where our relationship was tested. He knew he did me wrong, so he begged me to come back. He came to where I was and cried in my arms about how he knew he fucked up. I told him everything that's done in the dark comes to the light, so be honest with me. If you lie and I find out the truth later, we are done, I told him. He said okay. Were you with another woman? I asked. And he told me he was, but they didn't do anything. They just talked, and he fell asleep.

Of course, I didn't believe him, but I did forgive him. So, we promised to call each other twice a day when we were away from each other. So now, with him not calling me back, all kinds of things were running through my mind.

Still sitting on the bed, I looked up and saw Elle's phone lighting up. She had a text message. I picked up her phone and walked out into the hall to call Drake, hoping he would answer a number he didn't know.

Ring … ring … ring …

I hung up when I heard a familiar ring tone from the room across the hall. I called again and let it ring twice. The phone across the hall rang twice and stopped. My heart started beating fast.

Am I tripping? I thought.

I went back in the room. By that time, Elle was out of the shower and had already put on her clothes. She was about to brush her teeth when I stopped her and explained what I'd heard. We went out in the hallway, and I called Drake's phone again. Of course, the phone across the hall rang twice, but this time, he answered.

"Hello, who is this playing on my phone?" he asked in a loud, deep voice.

We ran back into the room and quietly closed the door so no one would hear us in the hallway. I asked him what he was doing.

"Nothing," he said, "just playing the game and was about to warm up a pizza."

I asked him why he hadn't answered my calls and texts. He said his phone was messing up. I acted like I believed him and played it off. He told me he loved me, and we hung up.

"He is lying," I said looking at Elle, "and whoever he was over there with must have been the call from last night. He was the reason why I was late to your house. When I went back inside for my phone, he was in the shower. I questioned him about it all. He told me it was Chris, his homeboy and gym buddy. I should have known better because of how late he got that phone call. I want to go over there, Elle," I said.

"And say what?" Elle asked. "You think he just going to open the door if he knows it's you?"

"I'll just pretend like I'm room service and hold some towels in front of the peephole."

We walked across the hall, covered the peephole with a folded towel, and knocked on the door twice, saying, "Room service."

A woman voice shouted, "Just a minute."

Elle and I look at each other. When she opened the door, it was Amanda. Elle and I looked at each other and pushed the door open. Elle grabbed Amanda by the arm and forced her out into the hall. I walked in and slammed the door. Drake was lying on the bed naked with a towel around his waist.

"Kerry!" He jumped up, in shock.

"Wow ... really, Drake?" I said, fighting back tears. "You in Texas with another bitch on my birthday. I guess I mean nothing to you."

"Baby, I'm so— "Drake was about to say, but I cut him off.

"Shut the fuck up, Drake. I don't want to hear nothing you have to say. Then you here with this bitch, and she don't like me."

"Amanda! You know Amanda?" Drake asked, shocked because he didn't know about our past.

"Yes, and I know she did this shit on purpose. But you ... you lied to me, and you did this same thing on my birthday last year. You have no respect for me, and you don't love me," I said, walking away. I turned back around and said to him, "If you would have answered the phone, you would have known we changed our mind about going to Atlanta. Instead, we came here. At home playing the game, about to bake a pizza my ass, you liar! She must have been the call that you didn't want to answer. I fucking hate you, Drake. You are so wrong!"

Drake couldn't say anything. He wasn't expecting to find me in Texas, or he probably wouldn't have come. As I went into the hall, I heard Amanda say to Elle, "I can't believe you take her side and lock me out my room! You will regret you did that!"

"Bitch, you know you wrong, and if KK kick your ass, I'm going to let her," Elle said, shaking her head and placig her finger on Amanda temple like she was checking her.

"Let that bitch go, Elle. She can't get a man of her own, so she gotta steal mine. Bitch, I wish you would try something," I said with my fist balled.

"You not gone' do shit, Amanda," she said with a smirk on her face as she walked back into the room.

I grabbed her by her hair and punched that bitch in her face.

"Now say something else," I said as Elle pulled me back into our room.

Amanda went back into her room, and I could hear her ask Drake why he hadn't come out to defend her.

CHAPTER 8

They Got Me Fucked Up

Amanda

"So, you're just going to let that happen? After you told me you love me? I thought what we had was special. I thought you really loved me! We been together for three years, and you had her with you all this time?" I asked, knowing very well he had been with her. Deep down, I was hurt because he did say he loved me, and I had started falling for him too.

But I felt even better when I saw how sad and mad, I had made Kerry.

Fuck that bitch. She made me her enemy when she fell asleep on my twin brother, I thought.

I looked at the man I had just given myself to all weekend long. I trusted that when he told me he loved me, he meant it.

"Shit!" he said angrily. "Fuck, fuck, fuck, fuck!" was all his angry ass kept saying as he stomped the floor back and forth with his hands beating his head. It was like I wasn't even in the room. I was happy that the bitch had found out, but not like this. I wanted to set his ass up my own way. How did she even know? The sound of his voice scared me when he grabbed me and said, "Did you set my fucking phone to block her calls? I know I wouldn't do that shit, and I know I didn't do that shit, so you had to. Hell, you knew all along who I was with, like she said."

"We grew up in the same neighborhood. You delivered to all our houses before. Don't act like you didn't know. That bitch killed my brother."

"She did what?" he yelled, looking at me all big eyed.

"Yes, she was in a relationship with my twin brother, and we all went to Myrtle Beach for spring break back in 2014. We were on our way home when she fell asleep on my brother while he was driving. After we all made a promise that whoever rode shotgun had to stay awake."

"That doesn't mean she killed your brother. He chose to drive. He knew he had all your lives in his hands. He should have been more careful," he said.

That's when the rage in me for her grew thicker.

How in the fuck is he going to defend her like that? We made a promise to each other.

"Yes, I can see why you blame her, but he should have woken someone else up to drive once he knew he was sleepy. You can't go around blaming people for your brother's mistake. He was the one who knew he was sleepy, so he should have pulled off the road and given the wheel to the person who was asleep the longest."

"So, what are you saying, it's my fault?" I asked with the worst attitude any woman could have.

"No, that is not what I am saying. All I'm saying is that he should have been a little smarter. Like I should have been by not fucking with you. I just lost the woman I love," he said, starting to pack his things.

"You said you loved me too, remember? Last night, before you fell asleep."

"I didn't mean that for you. I'm used to telling KK that I love her before we fall asleep," he said in an agitated tone.

"So, that's it? You're just going to leave me here? You're going to act like I mean nothing to you? Like I'm not in love with you and that I don't have feelings?"

"Amanda, you just said you don't care too much for KK and that you blame her for your brother's death. How could you mean what you say when you're just getting back at her for what you think she has done? You don't really love me if you could do something like that to another woman. You're not who I thought you were," he said as he headed for the door.

"Please, don't leave me! Please! I'm begging you. I do love you, and I do need you. I can be good, I promise. Just give me the chance to prove it to you. Please!" I said. I did not know I felt this way. I had blinded my feelings with so much hate in my heart that I felt lost after he slammed the door.

This bitch had me fucked up. I wish I knew which door to knock on so I could give them hoes a piece of my mind.

All I could do was cry. It felt like I lost again to this girl, and I wanted nothing more than to make her pay for all she had done.

I was going to get my revenge, and I was going to make them both suffer for what they had done to me.

Once again, I was a victim to the both. I didn't really hate Michelle, but by getting in between me and Kerry's fight, she just became my next victim.

Just wait and see what I have in store for little ol' Elle.

And trust me, she will never see me coming. As for Kerry, I want that bitch to hurt even worse than I did before. I'll let them think they have won, and then I'm going to strike like a poisonous snake. She is going to feel my hate, and I will show no mercy to either one of the bitches. You want to stand up for your girl? Then you can fall with that bitch too. All she had to do was stay out of it. I liked her for who she was. Now I was going to hurt her for who she stood with.

"She pulled me out of my own room so her friend could lock me out. This is not your fight, but since you want to make it one, I'm coming for you next."

I said all this while I was crying in the mirror.

"I promise, I'm going to hurt them bitches for making him leave me. Then I'm going to make him pay. I don't have a heart. My heart left me the day my twin died, and now they all are about to find out, starting with that bitch Kerry and ending with dumbass Drake. Mark my words, I am going to make them suffer."

CHAPTER 9

I Really Fucked Up This Time

Drake

Ilove my girl KK, but sometimes I want to be with other women. It's not that I don't love my girl or care about her feelings. But I'm a man, and a young one at that. I'm not ready to settle down. I don't want a relationship with these women. I just want to hang out and have sex with them. Half the time, I just want to see if they'll fuck with me. And they always do.

What can I say? I look good and have a damn good job. It all started back when I got my job at UPS delivering mail to people's houses. I would say that was about three years ago. I was a nineteen-year-old man with a good job plus benefits. Sometimes I think these girls were ordering items just so I could deliver to them. Whenever I showed up again, they'd come to the door with hardly any clothes on. After the third trip, I got a feeling I knew what was going on. You see, I used to work on the dock before I became a driver, and I could tell a few months later after picking up boxes every day that my muscles started getting big. This was on top of my training to be a firefighter.

Then I started going to the gym on my off days. It showed in the summertime, when I was wearing my short-sleeve shirts and shorts. It gets crazy around income tax time. Some women even tip me.

Two weekends a month, I train so I can become a firefighter. Although the money is good, I enjoy being independent working as a delivery driver.

KK and I have been together for three years, and she's a good woman. She reminds me of my mom. My dad cheated on my mom for five years, and one day, she couldn't take it anymore and left. My dad made up his mind to get his life together. He didn't want no other woman or to see my mom with another man raising me, so he went to her and asked her to marry him, promising never to lie or cheat again.

I guess I get it from my dad. I mean, I didn't like to see my mom's hurt, and she taught me not to be like him. But right now, I'm having fun. I won't always be like this.

There's a few side chicks I mess with on a regular. Their names are Summer, Candace, and Amanda. Summer has three boys, so I don't see too much of her, but when I'm hungry, she puts it down, and I puts it down before I leave.

She surprises me with Muscle Milk, protein bars, whatever she can think of to keep me around. She's dark skinned and wears her hair sometimes long and sometimes short, but it be on point no matter how she wears it. She doesn't work, but she gets child support from two of her babies' daddies. The other one got killed a year ago, so she gets a social security check once a month for her youngest child.

Candace is an RN. She works twelve-hour shifts. She been hurt by her first love, so she doesn't want a relationship. She just wants sex every now and then, when she feels the need. Which is cool with me. I don't have to worry about no jealous-ass female. She doesn't care that I have a girlfriend, so every time she calls, I try to make my way to her as soon as I can, sometimes in between deliveries.

Then there's Amanda, that sneaky bitch. Now normally I don't call women out their name, but the shoe fits her. I met her a week after I met KK. She ordered some things, and I delivered them to her. She answered the door in some thin-ass shorts, leaving me little to no choice but to want her. She had my attention on that nice round ass she had. We both were members at the same fitness center. I was going there first, and then she started coming. I think she was keeping up with the days and times I was going there so she could run into me. Yeah, she seems promiscuous, huh? You have no idea. Ha, she's a real handful.

She was already in shape, but she wanted to keep her body toned. She would always come over to where I was and do her squats, knowing all the guys would be watching. But I could tell she had a thing for me. One day at the gym, I was lifting weights, and she came over and asked if she could spot me. She had on tights and a sports bra. You could see the imprint of her kitty, and I could feel my manhood rising. Amanda was special to me. She was kind and down to earth and knew how to joke around.

When she asked for my number, I was a little hesitant at first. Thought she was probably the type to mess with a lot of dudes. I couldn't turn that down, though. After that, we became gym buddies and met up on a regular. Amanda was also my lover, and she would have been the one I made my main girl if me and KK didn't work out.

Of course, she couldn't have me whenever she wanted, and that pissed her off. But, she's still around and wasn't going anywhere until tonight. This bitch blocked KK and my other two hoes I fuck with. I was wondering why I wasn't getting any calls. But Amanda was looking so good this weekend, I really didn't want any interruptions anyway. But it wasn't that bitch place to go through my phone and block anyone. That's where she fucked up. If KK was able to call straight through, then I would have had Amanda meet me somewhere else. Now she's causing problems with KK, and that's who I gotta go home to face. I been doing good all this time. Kk might have suspected something, but she didn't know shit until I brought my ass to Texas.

When KK walked in on me and Amanda room, my heart dropped. I had just got off the phone with her, so I was not expecting things to go down the way it did. On top of that, I just lied and said I was at home. I know I was wrong, but I'm glad KK kicked Amanda ass, 'cuz this bitch should never have blocked her. Then to find out they knew each other! Amanda is a dirty bitch. I gotta look out for her 'cuz that bitch is crazy. Ain't no telling what she got up her sleeve. All she wants is revenge from KK. She went out the way to get with me to make my woman mad, and I fell for it.

I ruined KK birthday again, and she probably won't forgive me after this. I knew she had plans to go out of town, so I made plans to go out of town too, but I didn't think we would end up in the same state—and at the same hotel!

KK is a good woman, and I really don't deserve her in my life. Her love is pure, and when she loves, she loves hard. My mom loves her and always asking when we are going to give her some grandbabies—but after we get married, she would say.

I remember when I first met Kerry. I had delivered a package to her house. When she opened the door to sign for her package, she had the prettiest smile. I could tell she was excited her order came in. She didn't pay me no mind. She signed the device, gave it back without looking up, and went back inside the house. I wanted to tell her how beautiful she was, but she was moving so fast, the words wouldn't come out. I walked back to the truck, saying to myself, *Damn, what if she doesn't order anything else for a while? I might not see her anymore.* I sat in the truck for a few minutes, trying to decide if I should go back and knock on the door, and finally, I did.

I knocked on the door, and she opened it, and our eyes locked on each other. I was speechless, until she asked, "Is there something wrong?" I told her I couldn't get back in that truck and pull off without telling her how beautiful she was to me. She smiled.

"I usually don't do this while in uniform," I said, "but I would like to get to know you, if it's okay with you."

For a moment, I thought she wasn't into me, but then she said, "Sure, I would like that."

We went out to eat a few times and seen a couple of movies before she decided to come chill at my apartment. She wasn't trying to rush nothing. We were more like friends before we became lovers, and that's what made her different from a lot of women. She went to college and did her four years, and when she starts something, she finish it. After six months, she moved in with me. Three years later, we're buying a house. She handles her business: she works every day, cooks and clean, and keeps her circle small. She doesn't fool with too many women. She has male friends that she knows, but it's not like she calls them. It's more like, when I see you in the streets, we'll speak. She is a beautiful woman, inside and out.

I snapped out of my thoughts. I had to get it together.

I gotta beat KK home, but it's going to be four and a half to five hours before my plane take off. This shit is crazy. I never thought it would end like this—KK catching me in a hotel room half-naked. I'm calling and calling her, but she's not answering the phone.

I really fucked up this time.

We Meet Again

Michelle

I was playing with Tony's business card in my hand as I listened to KK cry from outside the bathroom. I felt helpless as a best friend. I wished I could make her feel better, but I know I couldn't. Hell, no one could. The heart is something that takes time to heal when it's been broken.

Looking down at the card I held in my hand, I thought should I give her some space. Should I call him so we can have dinner, drinks, and talk some more? I wanted to call him, but I knew my girl needed me, so I set the business card down on the table. Walking over to the bathroom door, I knocked once to see if she would answer.

"I'll be out in a minute. Just let me get myself together," she yelled through the door.

I calmly replied, "Okay," then walked back to my bed, and fell on my back, looking up at the ceiling as the drama played out in my head.

I had no idea Amanda could be so mean and cruel. Then again, I did. After she found out KK was liking her brother, she was even mad when she found out her brother friend Brad Wansley really liked on KK. Amanda had a huge crush on him.

Nobody knew she was upset about that but me. He eventually started to like Amanda once KK and Allen started talking more. She was so sweet when we were in grade school. Once we entered high school, she hung around only when she wanted to be around me. She stopped hanging out with KK and only talked to me if I was alone. KK really played my friend to the max.

Why does she feel some type of way about KK? She seems a little jealous to me, and my mother saw what I saw. I knew she felt some type of way when we came home from spring break. I just didn't think she would stoop this low to get back at KK for her own brother falling asleep. I mean, hold *him* accountable. Hell, he could have killed us all. Has she ever thought about that? No, she puts the full blame on KK. That's just wrong!

As the door opened, I sat up in bed to look at her to see what her emotions were.

She looked like she had been crying hard. Her eyes were puffy and red. I hated her feeling like this. I offered her a small glass of wine from the minibar while we talked. I let her get whatever she needed to off her chest.

Her cell phone kept vibrating. She kept hitting ignore. I knew it was Drake.

She looked up at me and said, "What are we doing tonight, Elle? Let's go to a bar and flirt. We don't have to get any numbers. We can just make conversation with men to take my mind off things. I don't want to think about this anymore. It's my birthday and I don't want to be crying all night."

"Okay, stepping out of our comfort zone a little bit," I said.

"We can have a few drinks—just to give us a little buzz," she added quickly, since she knew how I feel about drinking and driving. "Lord knows I need it," she said with a half-laugh to show she was not going to let them ruin her weekend.

As we headed to the rooftop, it was crowded, so we found a spot and chilled until we figured out what we were going to drink. I made one phone call and told her one drink and we are out.

It took the waiter a long time to make her rounds, so I just said, "Let's go to a real club to have fun." What she didn't know was that I'd just made reservations for VIP at one of the hottest spots in Dallas.

We hit the room up so I could do KK's makeup to make her look like she was ready to party and not like she had been crying all night. We slid into something a lot sexier and headed for the club. As we approached the bouncers and the doorman, he unhooked the rope and said, "Tell the cashier it's on me," showing us his name on his badge it read "Cory"

I already knew it was about to be lit. You two ladies look beautiful. I will be inside in a minute. Be at the bar so I can be the one to escort you two to your table. With you two beautiful ladies looking this good, the first round is on me."

We looked at each other and smiled. The night was turning around quickly, and by the crowd, we knew it was about to be on. As we headed to the bar, the guy that hooked us up walked behind the bar, grabbed a bottle of champagne, placed it in a tub of ice, and lit it up with a sparkler. He motioned us to walk behind him as he led us to a VIP table closer to the DJ booth.

I held on to KK's hand as we headed to VIP. He placed the champagne on the table and handed us the flutes. He popped opened the bottle and poured us all a glass. We toasted and drank. He whispered something to KK, then ran off. She smiled at me and said, "I'm glad we came."

Smiling back, I was happy because she was happy. She deserved to be in a good state of mind. Hell, it was her birthday weekend. Who wouldn't want to have fun?

We were dancing and singing in our seat to Yo Gotti and Niki Minaj.

"I tell all my hoes, rack it up, bring it back, back it up, fuck it up … fuck it up." everyone in the club was rapping these lyrics throwing their hands up feeling the music. Their where women backing their ass up against guys and some were showing off by twerking. Then it seems like almost all the females were twerking. The whole club was turned up.

"Well, hello, beautiful. Didn't expect to see you here," a deep voice that sounded somewhat familiar said.

I smiled and responded with a "Hi!" I reached over and gave Tony a hug. Then I introduced him to KK while we were still standing. With a big smile on my face, I was happy now that he was here, because he had been on my mind since I had seen him earlier.

The DJ was playing rap and R&B, and we danced at our table. I was feeling pretty good from the champagne, not knowing it can give you a real buzz.

I saw how guys were checking us out, holding their glasses in the air and toasting to us as we all had a good time. The club was filling up, and our bottle was getting low. Tony motioned one of the waitresses over to our table for another bottle, but the owner walked over and shook hands with Tony, and as I looked closely, I noticed that the owner was Cory.

"Oh my God! Cory, I didn't even notice it was you. How have you been?" I asked, happy and surprised.

"I knew it was you. I was the one who took your reservations. Tony was right beside me. He said he had just run into you at the hotel. I wanted to say something then, but I said I'd just wait to see you in person. It is really good to see you two again," he said. Looking over KK, he said, "I remember you too. You were with Amanda's brother. Sorry for your loss."

KK looked over at me and back at Cory and said, "Thank you. I'm better now."

In a flirtatious kind of way, he replied, "I can see that. You are very beautiful—all grown up." He had my girl blushing for real.

We enjoyed their company and the party of the club, as we danced and drank and danced some more. The DJ gave a shout-out to KK for her birthday. Time flew by. It was after four, and we weren't ready to throw in the towel, so Tony walked us outside the club and into a party bus. We had never been on a party bus before, and when we got on, it was just the four of us. The driver pressed play, and music filled the speakers. The lights dimmed, and we got the ball rolling with more drinks.

We drove for a few minutes and then picked up a famous singer and his entourage. He was surprised we were on the bus with him and made us promise not to speak about this night to anyone. KK told the dancers with him about her cosmetic line. I helped them with their makeup and advised them that the leggings they were wearing would be better if they were fishnet stockings.

We made a trip to a twenty-four-hour store, and I helped them put together an outfit for their upcoming show. They all liked it and thanked me for my fashion expertise and told me to call them once I graduated to become their stylist. They gave me all the numbers to reach them, business and personal.

"The bus's name was *Vegas*, and what happens in *Vegas* stays in *Vegas*," he said as he winked at us. Once we agreed, we partied hard all night. I would go into details, but hey, we made a promise.

The celebrity and the driver were cousins of Tony and brothers of Cory, so that was how we even got to see them to begin with.

Being women of our word, we kept our word. We enjoyed ourselves, and when we looked up, it was 7:00 a.m. The bus stopped us back at our hotel. Yeah, we were lit and couldn't drive. Cory asked for my keys so he could bring me my truck back to us after he sobered up. Any other time, in my right mind, I would have said no. That goes to show how messed up I was. Walking up to the room, Cory was basically carrying Kerry. The birthday girl had a night of her life. Tony had my high heels in one hand and my clutch in the other. He was such a gentleman. Hell, they both were. As we reached the door, Tony asked me to join him back in his room. I was in no position to say no. I told KK I was about to go with Tony. She pushed me out of the room, saying, "Good! It's been years since she been laid. You'll think she was a virgin!"

Embarrassed by her comments, I hurried out the room, slamming the door with her and Cory still left in the room, laughing at me together.

"Excuse her. She had a little too much fun," I said with a laugh, trying to play it off.

We reached the nineteenth floor and his hotel room door. I got nervous about going in. He placed his hand on the small of my back and directed me into his room.

I walked inside. He had a suite. There was a living room, bedroom, kitchen, and all. He walked to the back and came back with one of his T-shirts.

"You can wear this if you want to get comfortable. I'm going to get out of these clothes. I will return in a second," he said as he walked to the back.

I sat down on the sofa and waited for him to join me. We talked about a lot, getting to know each other. Then we watched movies. I think after the second movie, I fell asleep.

Waking up to the feel of lips kissing me, I opened my eyes. As I looked into his eyes, we began to kiss. His lips were so soft and full, and his tongue was sweet. We kissed one another, and the drums started beating loudly in my heart. I felt a tingling sensation all over my body, so I pulled away.

"I'm sorry," he said, unsure of what I was going to do next.

Looking him dead in his eyes, I wanted more, but I didn't know how.

He stared back into my eyes and kissed me again, this time a little more passionately.

I exhaled and kissed him back softly with a little more passion.

"You are sexy in every way," he said as he ran his fingers through my hair. "Wow, this is your real hair?" he asked.

"Yes, why do you ask?"

"Most girls do not wear their own hair."

"I always find beauty in my natural self," I told him.

"See, you are different from most women. You have a confidence about yourself. I could see that in you when I first met you on Spring break. I am lucky that I get to see you a second time around. I hope this time we stay connected," he said.

"I ..." I started, but I was at a loss for words.

We focused our attention back on the movie. I was finding it hard to keep my eyes open. With all the fun we'd had, I couldn't see how he had so much energy.

I yawned and stretched out my arms and legs. He asked if I wanted to go lie in the bed. I told him yes. He stood and grabbed me by my hand and led me to his bed. I climbed into the king-size bed and got under the sheets.

He closed the blinds and asked, "Can I join you? I promise I won't touch you if you don't want me to."

I smiled and said yes. He lay down and kissed me once more, then wrapped his arms around me, and we fell asleep. I knew then he was the one I had my eye on and who I wanted to get to know. I felt lucky and alive all at the same time. I wonder what happened to KK and Cory after we left. Did they fall asleep, or are they still kicking it? I didn't know. All I did know was that I was where I wanted to be. At the right place and at the right time, with the right person. So far.

CHAPTER 11

The Fun Starts Now

Kerry

When Cory and I entered our room, I plopped down on my bed, saying, "What a day." He asked if I enjoyed myself, and I said, "Because of you, my birthday turned out to be the best. I am so happy I could cry," I said.

"What's wrong, baby girl?"

"Yesterday afternoon, I found out my boyfriend was here in Texas."

"Oh, shit where he at?" Cory said, cutting me off.

"I didn't know. He was at this hotel, a room across from us, with another woman."

"Damn, baby."

"But you, you, Mr. Good Looking, made my night," I said as I got up and stumbled over to him as he leaned against the table.

"How long you been together?"

"Three years, and I've never cheated on him."

"Would you feel bad if you did it with me."

"I don't think so," I said, biting my lips. Hell, I was already tipsy and feeling abandoned in love. So, what the hell?

Cory removed his shirt and exposed his abs. My heartbeat started racing, and I felt myself getting wet. I could tell he noticed that, because it was outta control. He pulled my clothes off and started kissing on my neck. I walked backward to the bed, removing my bra and thong, all the while making eye contact.

"Damn, you're perfect," he said as he removed his pants and climbed on top of me.

He massaged both my breasts. I was blessed with big perky breasts, and if you didn't know me, you would have thought I had implants. Then he started sucking on them, going back and forth from one breast to the other. While his lips were on one nipple, his hand was rubbing the other. I was still tipsy, so what he was doing felt so good. I closed my eyes, feeling like I had sunk into another galaxy. My legs were slowly spreading, and I was lost in the moment. He grabbed my hand and directed it toward his erect penis. I felt how hard it was and that it had a curve to the tip. He whispered for me to put it in. As soon as his penis head touched my vaginal lips, it already felt good. I felt helpless. I didn't want this feeling to go away at all. I wanted this moment to last forever.

I kept yelling, "Oh God, oh my God, don't stop."

"Damn, ooh-wee. Your turn," he said, flipping me over while still inside. I got on top of him and was lost again in the moment. As I was riding it back and forth, he grabbed me by the waist and helped guide me. When he finally let go, he never took his hands off me. His hands just moved upwards toward my breasts, and he started massaging them from behind. My head tilted backward, and I was getting wetter and wetter, like the ocean.

"Damn, baby, I gotta cum. Slow it down for a minute so we can keep going."

I heard him, but I didn't hear him. I was right where I needed to be. His penis was still standing strong. Besides, he was hitting all the right spots. I was still going in the same rhythm. I couldn't slow down. I didn't want to slow down. I don't think I knew how to slow down.

"Oh ... shit. Oh ... shit," he shouted. Then his body went limp and relaxed.

Hearing how good it made him feel made me cum at the same time as him. I fell on top of his body with his penis still inside, and we both fell asleep.

There's something about being drunk and fucking. It makes bad sex good sex and good sex the bomb.

I woke up to a knock on the door and a lady's voice saying, "Room service."

Cory went out of the way to prepare a nice breakfast, made especially for me. He even had a white rose on the cart.

Reaching for my clothes, Cory asked if I would stay the way I was. He liked what he was seeing and couldn't stop telling me how beautiful I was. He was going to make me his, and I would never have to worry about another woman. He has his own club, and he wanted everyone to see my face by his side.

"All these women in Texas. Why me?" I asked.

"Because I know you—well, I know you a little bit—but I know enough to say you're a good woman. Ever since I rested my eyes on you back when we met in 2014. You've been hurt, and I've been hurt, and I just feel like you wouldn't hurt me, and I want to show you I wouldn't hurt you. I'm not going to lie to you, Kerry. I have cheated before, but that comes back around when you love someone, and they hurt you. You see how that feels when the shoe is on the other foot," he said, walking toward me, lifting the top off the plate.

I was just eating and listening. I was so hungry and into this food. It was so ... good. Everything he was saying sounded so good. I wanted to take him up on his word, but I didn't know what I was going to do about my relationship with Drake. I didn't really want him, but I did, but I didn't care, because I liked Cory and the way he put a smile on my face.

After we ate, we fell asleep.

It was evening when we finally woke up again. He woke me by sucking on my nipple, but then, my phone rung. It was Drake. I sent him straight to voicemail. Then I blocked him, just like he let that bitch Amanda block me.

"When are you leaving to go back to Arkansas?"

"Um … what's today?" I asked.

"Saturday"

"Later on, this evening," I said with no hesitation.

"What if I ask you to stay the whole week?"

"I gotta give my job two weeks' notice."

"Please," he said with his lips pouting. "What if I pay you for the days you take off?"

"I'm sure I can come up with something. I do have enough PTO time."

"I didn't ask you all that, and I don't want you coming out your pocket for nothing the whole time you with me."

"Cory, you make me feel special, and I really like you for that. But the moment you show me something different, I'm going to get as far away from you as I can. I did something last night I don't normally do, and I don't really know you. But I made that choice. I hope I don't regret it."

"Kerry, I promise you have nothing to worry about. I don't have nothing, so don't worry about catching anything. And I don't spend my money on just anyone. Hell, I don't normally do this myself. But after you told me what went down, I had to react quickly, because I know a good woman when I see one, and I know I can treat you better," Cory said, looking me in my eyes.

"Cory, I want to be—"

He cut me off.

"And I will show you, starting today. I got a whole week to blow your mind, so you won't even think about giving that nigga a second chance."

"More like third," I said.

"What? Aw hell naw, baby. You deserve better, but you'll see how a real man supposed to treat a real woman."

Well, I better call Elle and let her know I'm staying, I thought.

She didn't answer, so I texted her to let her know I was enjoying myself, I was fine, and Cory was showing me a good time. I wanted to know what she was going to do—if she was going to stay or leave. I just knew Cory would want me all to himself, but if she did stay, I wouldn't neglect her. I was hoping she was having fun with Tony, and it would be nice if she spent a little more time with him as well.

It took about ten minutes, but she finally texted back, Happy birthday, letting me know she was staying, so I let Cory know what the game plan was. He was cool with it. I just told him I was his all week but I still gotta fuck with my girl. He told me to see if they wanted to grab dinner since we slept most of the day away. He was treating us to dinner for my birthday.

"Cory, your phone hasn't rung the whole time we been together," I said, just realizing it.

"I'm a businessman, and I have a business phone, so my people know when to reach me and when I'm not at the club, which I usually am. But I pretty much know when to check in. I don't have a lot of women calling me, and I don't call them. I'm not involved with anyone, so there's no one special in my life right now. Well, I take that back. You are special. But I'm not letting anyone interrupt us, and I'm glad you not letting anyone interrupt us. I must be doing something right."

"Oh, yes! You're doing everything right. You just keep on doing what you're doing, handsome."

We both went to take a shower, and of course, it went down again, and it was amazing. It was good to know it wasn't just the alcohol; it was good with or without it. I wasn't just caught up in the moment. It was long, fat, and curved at the tip. Cory was packing. I was screaming before he put it in. All it had to do was touch my lips; it didn't even have to be inside yet.

The warm water was already feeling good to my body, and he had me bent over, grabbing my ankles while the water beamed on my back. It was hard and long, and he felt every time I squeeze my muscles, telling me, "Keep doing that." After I had enough of bending over, he put me up against the shower wall, letting the water run off on his backside while he rammed himself in me. I never wanted it to end. It's like he was my medicine and I needed it twice a day—sometimes more, depending on how I was feeling—for the rest of my life.

We finished taking our baths, and once we were done, we stepped out, and he started drying me off. Then he told me to go lie on the bed. He finished drying himself off, then came to the bed with lotion and started rubbing me down. I was shy, but I couldn't show it. I mean, Drake never showed me this much attention before.

"Do I make you feel uncomfortable?"

"Yes ... I mean no. I like what you're doing to me."

"Good, I want you to always feel comfortable whenever you're around me."

"I want that too," I said.

"Good, let's get dressed so we can meet Tony and Michelle in the lobby."

CHAPTER 12

Planning My Comeback

Amanda

I came back to my apartment to sit with my thoughts. I had been played by the man I was supposed to be playing and shamed by the girl I was going to seek revenge on. The only friend I had left was on the same side of the girl I wanted to destroy. Apart from that, there was Lisa Brown, who I hadn't talked to in a while. I needed time to think of how I was going to get them to pay. I remembered I wrote down all the women's names in his phone. I thought I should call her and add her into my devious little plan, tell her that he was not the man she thought he was, and we set him up at the gym. Or should I act alone? That way, no one would know it was me. She had to pay for the loss of my brother and my broken heart. I didn't care what God or anyone else had to say about it. Fuck them and their happy little life together. Once I was done, there would be neither happiness nor a life there.

Pulling out my laptop, I searched for the tracking device I had placed on his phone. I was not about to let him play me like I was nothing to him.

As it went on searching, I took a shower and got dressed. Afterward, I drove to Little Rock, my hometown, to see what damage I could cause.

I had left Arkansas soon as I finished high school, following Cory here to Texas only to find out he was the biggest whore on campus. There was no way in hell I was going to fall for his I-want-only-you trick again. My brother was right. He was some college jock looking for notches on his belt.

I miss my twin. It was days like this when I really counted on him to be there for me.

I cried in the shower about my life and how I felt I had been robbed. Pulling myself together, I went back to my laptop to see if his destination had been located. Like the genius I am, there was: Clinton Airport in Little Rock.

"Bingo!" I said as I packed my bags to take a long drive home.

"Hello, Little Rock. I'm on my way," I shouted out loud to myself.

As I drove in hellish traffic, I had nothing but my thoughts.

I thought about just saying fuck it and moving on with my life. As I replayed that moment over and over in my head, I wondered, Why me? What is so hard about me to love. Why did everybody hate me so much?

People on campus had love for me. They all were so nice and friendly, inviting me to parties and such. I'm not that hard to get along with. Just don't cross me and we are fine.

I wished I could start over and redo some things. This is what I had. This is the hand I was dealt.

Cory was good to me the first semester. When you saw Cory, you saw me. Then, suddenly, the cheerleaders started throwing themselves at him at the sorority parties he used to invite me to. He would tell them he was with me, but that did not stop their show. He stopped going once I pointed them out. I must admit, he was faithful.

Then the head cheerleader came after him during our first fight. She emailed me the video of them together, and that is when I called it quits.

He hurt himself during a game. Well, the other team fullback hit him hard on the field. That is what put him out for the rest of that season. All the girls left him once they noticed he wasn't the star of the team anymore.

Then, he oh-so-conveniently fell back in love with me, wanting to be faithful again once he realized I had loved him for who he was and not for what he was doing. But once Lisa told the hospital not to let anyone see her and Tony's baby, Cory told me to not be friends with her. I can't just get mad at her for the choice she made with her husband. So, he broke it off with me due to the lack of sympathy I had shown to his cousin Tony. Men are so typical, showing loyalty to everyone but their woman.

So, I planned to allow him to catch me with Drake, hoping he would want me back. But once I saw him watching us by the poolside, I was turned off by how scared he was even to approach us.

He was the only man I had been with until I started seeking Drake. I fell in love with Drake because he was such a sweetheart. He knew what to say and when to say it. A real catch. I see why Kerry was so in love.

What I didn't see was why he chose her over me. I was there with him, understanding things he would tell me. I helped him out when he needed money and all. I didn't understand how he could just throw me away after three years. Then again, I should have known better. After all, he had been playing Kerry the whole time they were together.

Although I was faking my feelings, I played a damn good role at being by his side every time he needed me.

So, he owed me answers and an apology. I wasn't going to leave him alone until I got it.

I didn't want a damn thing from Kerry. No number of apologies would make up for her falling asleep. We made a promise, and her disloyal ass broke it.

Michelle I could forgive if she stayed out of my way. Nawl, fuck that. She needed to get hers too. She was real and true to me. She would call and check up on me when I started college. She would send me money when I needed it. I can see why she would take up for her bitch of a friend. She is a good friend, just to the wrong person.

If she stands clear, then I won't hurt her. If she gets in my way, she is doomed. That's all I'm going to say about that.

I wanted to visit my mother, but I can't right now. I have damage to do, and she will just be a reason why I won't follow through with my plans. My phone beeped at the same time my open laptop did to notify me he was at another location. I was halfway home to Little Rock from Texas when I needed to fill up. I felt a little weak from being hungry. I hadn't had anything to eat since yesterday's drama.

Getting back on the road, I sat in silence—no music and barely my thoughts. I was on my way to do major damage to my haters, and I was ready to start with that bitch Kerry. I picked up speed because I had three hours left. Then I was ready to lay low and strike.

I had it all planned out. Classes for me didn't start back up until this fall, so I had plenty of time to get it all done.

As I approach the address located on his tracking device, I saw him getting out of the car. He had his hands full with his luggage. I waited for the cab to leave so I wouldn't be seen. I pulled up three houses away. It looked vacant.

Pulling out my cell, I dialed his number while keeping my eye on his house in case he left.

"Hello, why are you calling me?" he said in an irritated tone.

"Where are you? Can we talk?" I responded.

"Hell, no! I left to clear my head! I need time to think. Just give me some space to sort all of this out. You think you can do that for me?" he asked.

"Yeah, but how long do you think you need?"

"I don't know. I live with Kerry, and I think she needs me to explain myself to her. She needs to know how I feel. Damn, give me some space. I'll call you!" he said before he hung up in my face. I saved this address, because now this stupid-ass man just told me how I could find her ass.

Men are the dumbest human beings on this earth.

Just like that, I found how I could get to his precious little Kerry.

Time had passed, so I left. I had enough information to do anything I wanted, anytime I wanted, thanks to that dumbass boy.

Later that night, since I had nothing to do, I called Drake again. He just let it go to voicemail. I knew he would. Hell, he is so predictable.

I was in hiding and had to lay low. But he couldn't run too far.

I know where he lives.

CHAPTER 13

Our Day Together

Michelle

We fell asleep up under one another. It was a beautiful thing. I slept like a baby. It was 5:26 p.m. when I opened my eyes. I was about to move over when he gripped me tightly.

"Where are you going?" he asked.

I smiled and said, "Nowhere."

He opened his eyes, and we were face to face. There was something about the way he looked at me that made my heart skip beats. He told me, "You are so sexy when you are sleeping. I watched you sleep. I was kissing you, and you kept pushing my face away, but I just kept kissing you. You are so sexy, and I'll do whatever it takes to make you mine," he whispered in my ear.

My heart raced, and my focus was on the words he was saying to me. I'd never had a man tell me those things and mean it. DeWayne was my first and the only guy I had ever been with. He was older, and that is why I fell for his words. He was a clever man, real street and hotheaded. I only lost my virginity to him. He went to jail the week after, and I knew then he was not the one. I was so upset with myself, I just never looked at guys the same. I promised myself I would make sure he was for real the next time I met a man and gave him my body.

I'm not a weak woman, but I do believe having sex involves deep feelings and love.

"What's on your mind, sweetheart?" he interrupted my thoughts.

"You," I said, looking up at him.

"Oh, yeah? What was the thought?" he questioned.

"Whether you are for real or you just want my body."

I hoped that would not run him off.

"I can have any girl's body I want, and she could be here instead of you. I chose you. I'm here right now with you. Have I pressured you into anything?" he asked.

"No," I answered.

"Okay, then. I'm a man, baby. Sex don't excite me. A real sexy, beautiful, confident woman who knows what she wants— that's what excites me."

I sat quietly for a second, appreciating his comeback. He got in my face to look me in my eyes, and he kissed me, this time with passion and with his tongue. I kissed him back freely, no worries, no cares. He seemed for real, and I was willing to see how true he was.

"You have always been sexy to me. I used to think about you a lot after spring break. I told my mother about how I wanted us to be. I told her how I liked how you showed me attention. I knew something special was in you when you didn't sleep with me just to say you had sex. You know, a lot of girls chose to do that around that time—away from their parents hanging around other fast girls—but not you. You were different, and I prayed that I would see you again."

"Really? You took me to God in prayer?" I asked, feeling a rush in my heart. I never knew he saw all that in me in just a few days of knowing me. We did talk about a lot and related our values that our parents had set out for us.

"Yes, I am not the kind of guy you might be used to. I pray before I make life-changing choices. My parents are still together, and I admire their love. I seek that forever loyalty in a relationship. Anybody can have sex, but what's next? Is that all a woman can offer? If so, I don't want it."

Just listening to him had me thinking about a lot. He was right in everything he was saying. I understood that we were both looking for the same thing.

We both took our time to see what our life partner had to offer. This was music to my ears and a good feeling in my heart. I didn't know such a man existed until I ran into Tony again. He was going to be my knight in shining armor.

"You're in deep thought again," Tony said, breaking the silence that filled the room.

I just looked up at him and smiled.

Staring back down at me, he smiled. This time, I reached in for a kiss. I kissed him as if my lips were inviting him to do more.

"Mm looks like you're feeling me too, baby girl. I want more, but only if you want more. I don't want to rush you. But once I'm in, I'm in. You can trust that I will be in it for the long ride," he said in a baritone whisper, with a sexy smolder that made me melt.

He had me speechless. All I could do was kiss him.

Kissing me back, he lifted the T-shirt I had on and unhooked my bra, exposing my full breasts. He leaned back as the shirt fell over my body. Looking at me, he smiled a half-flirtatious smile and called me sexy. I fell for him the moment he grabbed me and asked, "May I, have you?"

Heart racing, with chemistry filling the air, I replied, "I'm scared."

He kissed me and pulled my body closer to him. "I won't hurt you, and I'll never take you for granted." He lifted the shirt over my head. Then he slid down my panties and said, "I promise, I know how to love. I can love you in all the right ways. You can trust me when I say my heart knows it's you that I want."

In a slow whisper I heard him say, "I need a woman touch as well as her true love."

I felt a deep connection as I felt that way too. I needed love and affection due to not having parents and a lover. I feel lost and alone in this world sometimes, so as for now. All I can do is live in the moment. And hope and wish he is the one this time.

He kissed and softly sucked on my skin as his hands caressed me all over my body.

"I have been with only one man, and we touched only one time. Please, be gentle with me," I told him as he handled my body with care.

"I'm going to take my time, and I'm going to make love to your body like you never felt before."

He pulled me down under him, looked deep in my eyes, and said, "Trust me, you are mine from this point on." I smiled because that was the only thing, I was strong enough to do. He placed his hand on my love and caressed me until I melted in his hand. "Mm, that's it, right there, baby," he said. I moaned loudly with the pleasure he was giving me. He rubbed his manhood over my wet love and stopped. Looking me in my eyes, he asked, "Are you ready?"

"Yes," I whispered in between heavy breathing.

He went down on me and made me feel so good, I moaned and squirmed. Holding my hips, he kissed my body part as if it were my lips, smacking out loud and talking to it as if it were going to respond.

"You are so sweet," he said, kissing me over and over. "You are so pretty," he said as he licked my love nest.

"Mm."

"Mm."

He kissed my love once more making me shiver. Then he rubbed his manhood over my love and slowly pushed his rod onto me, but my love hole was tight. He smiled and said, "It has been awhile, huh?"

Blushing from embarrassment, I covered my face.

He moved my hand and said, "Don't be ashamed. I like you just the way you are."

We kissed as he pushed it again inside me, and this time, a little went in.

"Oh," I moaned.

"It hurts?" he asked.

"A little," I said.

He kissed me and said, "I'll go slow, baby. I will be gentle."

He slowly pushed again, but it didn't go any further.

"Can I take the hat off until I get it in?" he whispered in my ear.

I asked him if that was a safe thing to do?

He laughed and said, "Yes, are you ok with it?"

"Yes."

We both laughed with full trust in each other.

"I meant what I said, baby. You're mine from this point on," he said as he pushed the tip in.

"Mm."

I moaned softly as he eased it in.

"Daaaamn!" he said, dragging that word in a low voice, as I let out a gasping moan. Once we had encountered one another for the first time. He pushed some more, and this time, my body combined with his, and we commenced making love.

He felt so amazing after my body waxed over his manliness. He stroked me softly and whispered in my ear how good I felt to him. Our lips met, and we kissed. The room felt as if it were spinning, and my body felt like it was floating on air.

"I can stay here with you forever," I said.

Softly stroking my body, he moaned and moaned.

"Girl, where have you been all my life?"

"I'm here now," I said in my sexy whisper.

We kissed, and our bodies moved in unison. He was all I wanted at this moment, and I had no reason to hold back.

As my bodied creamed at every stroke, he moaned at every burst. I had him inside me, and my body gripped him every time he pulled back. I had him weak, and he had me pleased.

He whispered in my ear, asking if he could stay in as he released.

Not wanting a baby, I told him to keep it safe until we made it official.

He pulled out and moaned loudly.

When he finished, he looked at me and said, "We are official. You belong to me now, and I belong to you. You are mine, and I am yours."

We kissed and stared at one another.

"How are we going to do this?"

"Do what?" I said.

"I don't want you to leave today."

"I don't know. I have to check with Kerry," I said as I reached for my cell phone on the nightstand. I saw I had a message and a missed call. I checked my text first, and it was KK. It read:

> Hey, I'm really enjoying myself, I am fine, and Cory is really showing me a good time. What are you doing? Because I really am not ready to go home just yet. I want to stay another week. How do you feel about it? I called my job told them I had an emergency and need to use my sick time. They were ok with it. Hit me back and tell me something. By the way I can use this personal time alone with Cory if you know what I mean.

After I read this out loud, Tony smiled and said, "I could really use time alone with you too. I know you have bills and a life to get back to. I can compensate you for whatever you need. I own my own business, and I am CEO of a football stadium here in Dallas. You know my cousin Cory owns his own club as well. I would love for you to let me show you how I treat my woman. Now, a week is not long enough, but it's a nice length of time to show you what you can look forward to."

I smiled and texted my girl back, "I'm game," before I told him I would stay.

We kissed and shared a hot shower. My phone buzzed. It was KK, asking us to join them for dinner. It was her birthday, so why not?

We talked a little longer, and then we headed over to my room so I could put on some better clothes. That way, we all could have dinner and chill while we all hung.

CHAPTER 14

Praying for Her Forgiveness

Drake

It has been two days since I last seen my woman. I have been calling her and calling her. She just hit ignore on me every time. I hate myself for what I have done. She doesn't know that I do, I really do, love her. I just need to hear from her. I swear, I never meant to hurt my KK. I never intended for her to see me with another woman.

If I could turn back the hands of time, I would have just stayed my ass at home. Waited on my baby to walk through that door to kiss, hug, and shower her with my love.

I know I fucked up this time. She would have called me by now.

My mind was full of thoughts and memories of that day.

"Damn!" I yelled out loud, mad at myself. "How could I be so damn stupid and not cover my tracks?" I asked myself as I flipped the channels on the TV. I paced the floor back and forth as I waited for her to pull into the driveway. My nerves would be at ease if she was here, walking around mad and not talking to me. I could handle that. It's her being gone and mad that is driving me crazy.

I picked up my phone to call her again, and this time it went to voicemail. I got so mad, I threw the phone, cracking my screen.

"Fuck!" I cursed myself as I looked at the broken state my phone. Now I needed to get me a new phone.

"I never should have left Dallas!" I yelled out loud.

I grabbed me a shot glass and poured me a shot. Hell, before I knew it, I had drunk almost the whole damn bottle. Yeah, I was fucked up, but I couldn't be mad at nobody but myself.

I had fallen asleep on the sofa, still buzzed from my earlier drinking. I looked at my cell phone to see if I had missed her call or text. Nothing. I dialed her number to see if she would pick up and to leave another message for the thirtieth time. This time her phone didn't ring. It just sent me to voicemail. I tried to leave a message, but her mailbox was full.

Now I was starting to get pissed off.

"She knows I'm trying to call her, and I know she received my messages. If this girl on her way home, she had better have a good reason for ignoring my call. No matter what, I am still her man, and we do live together. She must come home today because she has work tomorrow."

I texted her phone, but it said the message couldn't go through. Now I was starting to get the feeling she had me blocked. As I looked over the texts, they all said, "Sending."

I never had so many emotions go through me all at one time. It had me going crazy. I took a shower and played a video game to kill time and take my mind off her.

When my cell phone rang, I jumped just to see if it was her. I hurried up and hit ignore when I saw Amanda's name pop up on my broken screen.

I noticed then I had to get out of this house.

"Chris," I said when my boy answered my call.

"Man, I need to get out of this house. Where you at, man?" I asked.

"On my way to the gym. I have drill next week, so I was getting an early start. Meet me at the fitness center right now," he said.

He doesn't know what went down. Hell, he doesn't even know about Amanda, Summer, or Candace. I had to tell somebody. I had to get this off my chest. I needed advice, and I needed it now. I changed my clothes, grabbed my gym bag, and headed to the fitness center. I blasted my music the whole ride there, giving myself the peace of mine to deal. I had no idea what this woman was thinking or doing. When I reached the parking lot, my cell phone rang again. It was Candace.

I told her I was busy, and I would call her later. Then I walked into the gym, ready to meet my boy and tell him everything.

"What's up, man?" I said as I approached him.

"Big D, what's good, homie?" he replied with a handshake.

"Man, too much I can't call. I need your advice about some things. I just need you to listen now and ask questions later."

"Dude, it sounds like you bring drama by how rough you look. Okay, I got you. Just get it off your chest."

We conversed as we stretched.

"I'll spot you while you talk. Then after you spot me, cool?" he said.

"Cool," I replied.

We worked out, and I told him everything from front to back. He looked at me, surprised that I would even step out on Kerry. He knows she's a good woman for me, and he was a little upset about it. I can see why. I knew better than to be doing this stupid shit on her. Now I'm paying for it. I keep replaying the look of hurt on her face. I keep replaying it repeatedly.

"I fucked up this time man I feel it. I did, man, I really did," I told Chris.

He just sat on the weight bench, shaking his head like he knew it too.

When we finished with our short workout, I headed to the house to see if KK was home. Words could not explain how my heart dropped when I saw she still wasn't there. Walking into our house had never felt this damn empty.

Pulling out by phone, I called my baby again. Again, it went to voicemail on the first ring.

I poured myself a shot, just wanting to be in another world right now. I needed to talk to one of my parents, but I knew better. They were going to drill the shit out of me. Both my parents love KK like one of their own. I had to sit in my own shit this go-around. But I knew I was going to do whatever it took to get her back in my good graces. No doubt about it, I was going to have her in my life, no matter what I had to do. She was mine, and I had to prove this time around, harder than ever, that I was hers.

My cell phone buzzed, and I hurried to it, thinking it was KK.

"Shit, this bitch doesn't understand English, I see," I said out loud. I read the text Amanda had sent, asking if I was still in Dallas.

I just left the message unanswered. She was crazy if she thought I was tripping over her. I'd answer her when I felt the need to. Until then, I need to figure out how I was going to ask Kerry for her forgiveness.

I wanted to do something special for Kerry, something that would put a big smile on her face when she walked through the door. That's when I thought about roses. Women love roses, I thought to myself as I pulled out my phone to search a nearby flower shop. I was going to have the house covered in roses and present her with a ring, asking her to marry me. I called to see how soon they could have it delivered the next morning.

After that, I went by the jewelry store to shop for a ring. Good thing I had saved up for this moment. With my apology and a proposal right alongside it, she had no choice but to say yes.

I left the house to go the mall to find the ring I knew she would say yes to. With the plan I had, it couldn't do nothing but work. I was on my way to set this up by the morning so that when she came in from work, the house would be covered in roses with a ring right in the middle of the table.

She was my baby, and I knew at this moment that I was ready for commitment. I just hoped she believed that I was for real this time.

After looking over the rings and talking to the dealer about carats, I got her a 3-carat two-piece gold engagement ring. I talked the manager down to a great deal. I paid $13,457.99 up front and told him I would have the rest paid off in three months. I could have paid for the whole thing, but we talked about payments, which sounded good to me. I had gone and preordered the roses to arrive around 1:30 p.m. the next day. That way, when she came home, everything would be set up.

I was going to get my baby back if it was the last thing I did. I had to make it right with her and with us. She was going to be mine for the rest of my life, and I was willing to prove to her how sorry I was.

I hated that I had hurt her, and she was going to see how I regretted the poor decision I had made being with Amanda. I was going to call Candace and cut all ties with her too. I couldn't go on treating the one who been down with me since day one so poorly.

I was ready to be the man she needs. I had a good feeling about this, and I knew in my heart she would want this from me.

I was ready for her when she got home tonight. I had cooked dinner and opened a nice aged bottle of wine. Not wanting to upset her tonight, I planned to just make her dinner and give her time to think.

I looked at the time: 8:50 p.m.

I sat by the window, waiting for her to pull in at any moment. I was ready to see how things were about to go. I waited by the window until I fell asleep.

CHAPTER 15

Posted Up Waiting

Amanda

He can't keep running and hiding from me, ignoring my calls and my text messages. I wasn't having it, and he had me fucked up. So, I went to my favorite spot on his block and watched his house. I followed him to the gym, where he met a guy, and I watched him work out with him.

I didn't like when he went to the jeweler. Like, what business did he have there? I know he not about to propose to that bitch! Not after being all freaking and in love with me. She would be a dumb bitch to say yes.

I didn't want him to know I was in town, so I just lay low, going unnoticed. I was wondering, why hasn't Kerry showed up yet? Was she really that upset not to beat his ass home? Hell, that must have been one hell of a flight. I beat both their asses here. What the hell? I just wanted to do my damages and get the fuck out of Dodge. But these two ass-backward-ass folks are unpredictable.

I started to hit his ass in the parking lot, but that would have gotten me caught up. Too many witnesses around. I had to do my dirt on the low.

He so weak. What in the hell was I thinking, fucking with this nigga? To think I gave him my body without a rubber. He knew how to fuck me good and tell lies. That's why his ass is in this predicament now. He gon' learn by me. I don't play when it comes to my heart. You better ask about me. I can be a crazy bitch if you push the wrong buttons.

Anyway, I was just sitting outside his house, waiting for his precious Kerry to arrive just to show her how dirty of a man this motherfucker was. All in my hot box raw, and he all in love with her. Shit, I can't tell. Four hours had passed, and it was getting late. I had a feeling I was wasting my time tonight.

Not really feeling this stakeout, I rolled out. By the looks of it, she wasn't coming home tonight, and if so, it was too late for me to be sitting in front of this for-rent house.

Before I left, I called him once more to see if he was going to answer.

I got his voicemail, and it was my last time calling for the night. I had enough time to do whatever it was I wanted to do.

I called me an order in, because he had me so fucked up, I hadn't eaten.

I bought me a bottle and went to the room just to chill. I was going to give him a couple of days. Then I was going to call. If he didn't answer this go around, I would set my plan in motion to do him in and leave. I'd come back for Kerry when that bitch got home—if she came back. She just might be smart enough to kick his ass to the curb. I know I was soon—just as soon as I left my mark to teach him he shouldn't fucked with my feelings like he did with his other whores.

So, both they ass had time to do all they needed. It was only a matter of time before I sought my revenge. I'd pour gasoline around their little want-to-be-perfect-ass home and set that bitch on fire. They don't need to fuck with me.

On my way to my room, I saw a cutie placing his card in the slot.

"Hey, handsome, need help putting it in?" I said with a half-smile on my face when he looked at me.

"I think I got it, pretty lady. You alone here?"

"Yes, why do you ask?" I replied.

"I am too, and I went out tonight looking for some company. I didn't find anyone worth bringing back. You look like you can keep me in good company. Wanna join me?" he said.

"How long are you here in town?" I asked.

"One week for business. I'm a former detective, and I work for national security. I help set up systems and video cameras for residences and business as well. I'm also here for a little pleasure," he responded.

"Former detective, huh? Why did you quit?" I asked.

"I still hold the title. I'm working to start my own office."

"Well, how about we go to dinner tomorrow when the sun goes down and see if we reach the point of nightcaps," I asked, not feeling up for company tonight.

"Sure thing, sweetheart. I'll take you up on that offer. I'm Jeff, by the way."

"Hi, I'm Amanda. Nice to meet you."

"You have yourself a good night, Amanda."

"You do the same."

We both entered our respective rooms and called it a night.

I was willing to go on this date, but we were going to eat here, in this hotel. Little did he know, I was not trying to be seen by no one. I hope he understands, or our plans are off. I wasn't in town looking for love. He was fine and all, but I have shit to do. So, he must understand. I fell asleep as soon as I filled my stomach. I watched Drake all day, trying to find out all his business while waiting to approach Kerry by herself. See how tough she is alone. Yeah, I'm no idiot. I knew Elle was going to help her friend fight me, like she said she would.

I wanted to see her hit me again while we were alone, just us two. I been waiting to whoop her ass for years.

Morning came, and I wasted no time snooping around Drake and Kerry's home. I was surprised to see she still hadn't showed up. What had she gotten herself into in Dallas that had her still out of town. Or was she here, just at Elle's house? I didn't have an address for Elle. All I had was this empty-ass rental house driveway to sit in and wait for her ass to come home. She had a life there, so I knew she had to come back sooner or later.

In the meantime, it was getting close to my dinner date with what's-his-name.

I pulled out and drove off to my destination to have dinner and a convo.

When I arrived back at the hotel, I rushed to my room to get ready. I'm glad I packed me something elegant to wear. I had this nice navy-blue peplum-hem cocktail dress. I brought it just in case Drake came to his senses. It hugged my body and complimented my ass. After I freshened up, I gave myself a little glance in the mirror before he knocked.

We dined and had a great time. He was from New York and loved the calm, slow of the South. The hospitality was better than the city, I guess. Anyway, we had more things in common than I thought. Time had snuck up on me, and before I knew it, it was after nine.

The waiter brought us another bottle of wine, and we enjoyed our time. We related on a lot of hot topics about so many things going on around us.

He almost made me forget my whole mission of coming back home.

Having someone who understands me is a big plus in my book.

Not wanting to move too fast in whatever it was we had going, I refused his offer to go back to his room. He begged to differ, and I gave in. Who was I kidding? I was having fun, but not enough to sleep with him tonight. I had shit I needed to do, so I gave him my time, not my body.

When I opened my eyes to this new day, I was ready to do everything I had come to do to get back to Jeff. He was on my mind before I fell asleep. If he kept this up, I might just be Mrs. Jeff, I said to myself.

Turning on my laptop, I searched for Drake on the tracker I had in his phone. It read that he was still at home.

I got ready to make my move. I would sit and wait until it was my time to strike. I left the hotel with a different kind of feeling about today.

I stopped and picked up breakfast before I headed over to see what Little Miss Kerry and Dumbass Drake were up to.

As I arrived, there was still no sign of Kerry. I had to wonder, was she giving up on him? Better yet, was she just giving up on coming home?

"Now, do not get me wrong. I don't like the bitch, but damn, Drake, she doesn't even want to come home!" I said my thoughts out loud. Then I laughed at this stupid-ass man I had fallen in love with.

I had a bad feeling about her still being in Texas. I knew Michelle had run back into Tony, so I wondered if Cory had seen them together. I gave it a quick thought but paid it no never mind.

Did she have someone down there she had eyes for?

Or was she in hiding at Michelle's house?

I didn't know, but I called Drake's phone to see if he answered.

"Hello," he answered.

"Hey, what are you doing?" I asked him.

"Nothing shits, just chilling. What are you doing?" he asked.

Now, I had no idea he was going to be nice or even answer his phone. I had a chill go through my back, as it felt like the old us.

"I miss you," I told him.

"Do you? I miss you too," he said in a deep voice.

"Are you back home?" I wanted to know.

"Yes, I came back to talk to KK to see if she would forgive me," he said.

"What will happen to us if she does?" I questioned.

"I don't know, Amanda. I really don't know. I didn't think I had these types of feelings for her. When she came in on us, I seen how bad I hurt her. It made me feel some type of way, you know? I never had deep feeling for her because she had always been there for me. I guess I took advantage of her because she was so good to me," he went on to say. "She has never made me question her love for me, but I have always been playing with her love. Now that I can't see or talk to her, it has me ready to be the man she needs me to be."

I asked, "What about us? Do you have feelings for me?"

He answered, "Yes, Amanda, I have feelings for you, but I love her more. What me and you do is fun and all, but when KK said you knew about us, that made me see you differently."

The conversation got quiet, and we both just sat there, breathing through the phone.

Breaking the silence, I told him, "I don't want nobody else but you. If you find out what it is and who it is you want, will you at least be upfront with me?"

"Yes, Amanda. I can do that. Just give me time to sort all of this out. I do love you. I'm just confused about who I want to be with right now," he said.

We said our goodbyes and hung up.

I had the answer I needed now, but I wasn't sure he was for real.

I needed time to clear my head, so I headed back to my room to think some things over.

I had a crazy feeling about Kerry still being in Texas, or still being gone for that matter. I let out a sigh of relief after talking to Drake. When he said she hadn't come home, it made me wonder why. Most women would hurry home to sort out all their dirty laundry.

Why was Kerry still in Dallas? That was the million-dollar question.

I reached for my phone to call my girl to tell her I'd seen Michelle run back into Tony. This would be my payback for her ass pulling me outside my room. I know Lisa going to check her about her husband, Tony. I became friends with Tony's wife while we were in college, when Cory and I were together. I had to let her know, since I'd seen those two together at the bar at his hotel the night, I was trying to make Cory jealous by being with Drake. I was going to set Lisa up to find Elle and Tony together, since she wants to get in between Kerry and my fight.

I had it all planned for Cory to find Drake and me. That was what I'd had planned the whole time, until I saw how scared he was even to approach us. I was having way too much fun with Drake, but Little Miss Perfect fucked that up when she barged into our room and sent Drake home crying like a little-ass baby. If it wasn't for her using Elle's phone, she never would have caught us. Elle seemed to have her hands in everything, so let's see how she get out of this one. If they thought I was a crazy bitch, they really don't know who Lisa is. Oh, but they are about to find out.

While this boy getting his shit together, I need to lie low to see what the hell is going on.

CHAPTER 16

Birthday Dinner

Kerry

As I stepped out of the elevator, holding hands with Cory, I saw Michelle and Tony relaxing in the lobby. She was sitting on the couch, and he was sitting on the armrest, bent over, talking to her with a smile on his face. When they saw us approaching, they stood up and walked toward us.

"Hey, Tony."

"What's up, Kerry. You doing all right"?

"Yeah, I'm good. Can I borrow my friend for a few minutes," I said with a smile on my face, not waiting for an answer but grabbing Elle's arm at the same time?

We walked over by the bar to talk about our plans for the week.

"Look, I'm checking out tonight. Besides, I'm ignoring Drake's phone calls, and I don't want him popping up here, so I'll be at Cory's place for the week."

"Okay, cool, because Tony is staying here temporarily, so I'll be staying in his suite. If Drake does see my truck up here, he won't know what floor. I don't care if he run into me. I'm not telling him shit."

"Okay, let's get back to the guys. I'm ready to eat. We can talk about them on the ride home."

We walked over to the guys to see if they were ready. Of course, they were eager to have us by their side.

"Are you guys ready to eat?" Michelle said, looking at Tony.

"Why, yes, we are, huh, Cory?" Tony said, licking his lips and looking at Elle as if she were dessert ready to be served.

"You bet," Cory replied, his gaze never leaving mine.

"We are too," Michelle said.

"What did both of you have in mind?" I asked.

"We are going to this spot called Dakota's Steakhouse," Cory respond.

"Sounds good. Let's go," I said.

"Are we riding together?" Tony asked as we walked to the parking deck.

"No, sir. Different cars, lil' buddy. We are going home afterward," Cory said, winking at me, then grabbing my hand and walking toward his Range Rover.

It took about ten minutes to get to the restaurant, Michelle and Tony following behind us. He was on the phone the whole time, talking business about his club. On slow nights, he doesn't need to be there too much, but he probably would been if I wasn't here. Friday and Saturday nights, he must be there; those are the busiest nights, and a lot of money and big faces are in there. Cory said we're going shopping this week. He wants me to be the best dressed and at his side the whole time. He said he don't want to have to beat a nigga ass for grabbing my ass.

We finally parked got out and waited for Tony and Michelle to meet us at the door. I was wearing a short black dress. Cory was wearing a pair of white Levi's and a black Gucci shirt. Tony was wearing Coogi, and Michelle wore a sexy royal blue romper. The waitress welcomed us and walked us over to our table.

"How many for tonight?" the waitress asked.

"Four."

"Right this way."

We followed the waitress as she switched back and forth. She was white with curves. She was built like a black woman, with short hair. I looked over at Cory to see if he was watching her ass, but instead, he was looking around checking out the restaurant. He's nothing like Drake, I thought. Tony and Cory pulled out our chairs for Michelle and me to sit.

"May I get you something to drink?" the waitress asked as she passed out the menus.

"Yes, a bottle of your best wine," Cory said. "By the way, today is my baby's birthday, so make that two bottles of your finest wine," he added.

"Coming right up," said the waitress as she walked to the kitchen.

She came back with both bottles and a fruit salad for everyone, and then she asked for our orders.

"I'll take a ribeye with asparagus and a loaded baked potato," Cory said, handing the waitress back the menu.

"I'll take the same thing he's having," I said.

Michelle ordered filet mignon, steamed broccoli, and Brussels sprouts, and Tony had the special surf and turf, which was Maine lobster tail, roasted wild mushrooms, broccolini, shrimp cocktail, and mac and cheese. We all looked at him.

"What?" Tony replied after looking up to see all of us staring at him.

"You gon' eat all that, fam?" Cory asked.

"Hell, yeah. I don't know about y'all, but I brought my appetite with me," he said, handing the waitress his menu.

We finished eating, and we were all full. All we wanted to do was shower and relax, but instead, we went for a walk in the park—Michelle's idea. Cory and I walked hand in hand, and Tony and Michelle were ahead of us, walking hand in hand too.

"Look … look … look," I said softly.

"Yeah, that boy in love. Michelle seems like a good woman for him, though."

"She is, and besides, she needs a good man in her life. She has been single for a while, so it's time. I'm glad he makes her smile and laugh. It'll be nice to see how things turn out between them."

"What about us?" Cory said, stopping to face me.

As he said that, my phone started ringing. It was my mom. I excused myself and walked in another direction to take my phone call.

"Hello."

"Kerry."

"Hey, Mama."

"Hey, baby. Drake been here. He wanted to see if I've heard from you. He told me what happen and said that he really hurt you, and he understand if you don't want to be with him anymore. He said he will have no choice but to respect your wishes. He only wants to talk."

"Mama hold up. There's nothing for me and Drake to talk about. He got caught—that was the last straw. When I go get my things from the house, if he's there, he can talk while I'm packing, but when I'm done, I'm gone. There's nothing he can say or do to change my mind."

"Kerry, I know how much you love that boy, but you got to do what's best for you, baby."

"I know, Mama. Next time he come back, don't answer the door, and if he calls, don't answer."

"Okay, baby, I love you, and be safe."

"I love you too, Mom."

I walk back over to Cory. He was standing there talking to Tony and Michelle.

"Everything all right, baby?" Cory said.

"Yeah, that was my mom checking up on us."

"Okay, cool. Yawl ready to split?"

"Yeah," everyone said at once. We all said our goodbyes, and I told Michelle I'd text her with the address, just so she'd know where I'd be staying. Our plans weren't to split up, but we felt safe, and it wasn't like they were strangers, so we were living life, having fun.

We made it to Cory's house, a nice long one-story house. It had a three-car garage with two already in it. We went in through the garage into the kitchen. It was huge. Cory said he loves to cook. That made me smile, because I love a man who can cook. We could be in here cooking together, I thought to myself.

We went out the kitchen into the dining room, which had a glass door that let you see into the backyard. No curtains were up, so you could see the pool. There was a private fence, so you didn't have to worry about anyone peeping in. He showed me the living room. It was big, with a large fireplace and a 90-inch flat screen on the wall above it. He even had a white polar-bear fur rug spread out in front of it so you could sit in front of the fire.

As we walked toward the rooms, the hallway was the longest I'd seen, and you needed to turn a corner to get to his room. There were four bedrooms and three baths. His bedroom had a California king bed, a dresser, and a 60-inch flat screen on the wall. He even had a mirror on the ceiling over the bed. Each room was decorated with furniture.

Cory said when he and his ex-separated, he had gotten all new furniture. He didn't want anything to remind him of her.

"Since you're going to be here a week, I don't want you living out of your suitcase. Tomorrow, we're going to put your clothes in the dresser over there," he said, pointing. "But right now, we 'bout to shower."

"Okay," I said, heading to his bathroom, which had a shower and a Jacuzzi. It had twin sinks, his and hers, and an extra closet full of dress shoes, casual shoes, and Jordan's. It also had a 40-inch TV in there if we didn't want to miss the news or just wanted to sit in the Jacuzzi watching a movie. We showered like we did at the hotel, but it was more intense. Cory had me up against the wall, pulling my hair, telling me it was mine if I wanted it. That went on until the water started getting cold. When that happened, we finished up quickly under the cold water.

Once we got out of the shower, I stretched out on the bed naked just so I could admire my body in the ceiling mirror. Cory came to the bed and told me to keep my eyes on the mirror. He told me to get it wet by playing with myself. I can't lie. I was even turning myself on, feeling myself getting wetter and wetter till I moaned. Then he started kissing me from my toes up to my vagina, and that's when I burst out crying. He gave me the best head I've ever had, and I was watching him in the ceiling until I came all in his mouth. I passed out.

I woke up to the smell of bacon. I looked over on the floor and found a T-shirt of Cory's to put on. I walked to the kitchen, where Cory was pouring us a glass of orange juice.

"Smell's good in here."

"Good morning, sexy."

"Good morning, handsome," I said, smiling as I walked toward him, giving him a kiss on his lips. "I can get used to this," I said, stretching my arms out, yawning.

"You haven't seen nothing yet."

"Every time you say that, you make me smile, and it's cause you want to see me happy. That's how I want to feel, and it's how I feel when I'm with you."

He looked at me and smiled. I went over to the table and sat. He followed with my plate and juice in his hand. I waited for him to sit so I could say a prayer before we ate.

"So, what did you have planned for us today," I asked.

"I figure we could stay here today to get to know each other with no interruptions. We can watch movies and go for a swim in the pool."

"But I don't have a swimsuit," I said.

"You don't need one. Just jump in naked." He smiled as he put a piece of bacon in his mouth.

"No … I can't do that."

"I'm just playing. Just wear your bra and panties. You won't be needing it no more today anyway. And besides, we can wash them when you're finished."

"Okay."

"We are going shopping before the weekend anyway, so we'll just pick you up a few of them."

"Shopping! What exactly do you have planned for us this week?"

"Today and tomorrow we just gon' chill here. I want as much personal time I can get with you, just talking. I want to read you. I want to know what you like and what you don't like.

What makes you happy or sad. What's your favorite food and color? Things like that, baby."

"Okay, okay, sounds good," I said, smiling from ear to ear.

"Wednesday, we're going to hit up some casinos and find a nice restaurant to go to. I'm not sure about Thursday, but we will be shopping all day. Sleep morning Friday. Then Friday and Saturday night, we're going to the club. Those are our busiest nights, so I gotta be there to promote and to make sure my money being handled right."

Our week went as planned. Wednesday, I won $200 at the casino. He didn't win anything. We ate while we were there. Thursday at the mall, we had so many bags. We went to the car at least three times because we couldn't carry them all. He wouldn't even let me bring my purse in, but I did sneak my credit card in, because I wanted to buy him something. He took me to the jewelry store and had me get my ring finger fitted, but he bought me a necklace instead. I think he tried to play it off, buying the necklace. I think he's preparing to make plans, I thought. We took pictures in the photo booth and had ice cream and a sandwich from Chick-fil-A. After the mall, we went to a few outlets stores before we went back to his house to relax. We had been on our feet all day, so he offered to soak my feet in Epsom salts and gave me a foot rub.

When Friday and Saturday finally came, we were at the club all day making sure everything was in order. Both days, I wore a sexy short dress, and Cory made sure I never left his side. He wanted to be seen with his future wife by his side. That's what he said. I'm not the club type, but it was jumping both nights.

I didn't know if I could get used to this, but the money was looking good. Besides, I loved all the attention and getting spoiled. I knew I would have to make up my mind soon. Not about Drake, 'cause that was a done deal, but as far as me being with Cory. That meant I would have to move here to Texas.

Sunday is tomorrow, and I know it's going to be hard to say goodbye. I just want to be with him all the time now. He makes me so happy. Too bad I can't send for my things in Arkansas.

CHAPTER 17

You Make Me Feel Brand New

Michelle

We finished dinner with KK and Cory, and then we all took a walk downtown at a park. We just talked and laughed over the things we liked and had in common. He was a breath of fresh air and a new thing, like a new bag or nice, comfortable 6-inch pumps. I needed what he had, but I didn't want to seem desperate.

I asked if he had any children. He said he lost a child to stillbirth. I felt sadness come over him, so I sat quietly with him as we walked the sidewalk.

"I never talk about it because it still hurts. The mother of my lost child blames me for some reason. I don't understand. You know, I wasn't finished with loving her. But after we lost our baby girl, she became distant, pushing me away, asking me for a divorce, and hating me for walking away. I needed her, and she wanted nothing to do with me. We were the happiest couple until our big loss. We became two people who hated each other. I didn't want another woman until I got over her, but you were at the bar, looking beautiful with all this long hair, and I wanted you—not in a sexual way, but to be with you, having you on my arm. I wasn't going to approach you, but I realized I knew you, and that's what made it easier. You are one beautiful woman, inside and out. I just knew you had a man."

He pulled me closer, facing me to him. "I'm glad I ran into you the second time around." We kissed, long and passionately, as he hugged me tightly.

We pulled away, and someone passing by yelled, "Get a room!"

We looked at one another, surprised, and laughed. Must have felt the passion between us to have yelled such a thing. *It is moments like this I can get used to*, I thought. I hoped he wouldn't change. I know things happen and no one is perfect. It's the connection that I'm seeking forever.

"Can we go back to your room and finish this later. I love talking with you, getting to know you, and just being around you. I am really enjoying myself with you. Never felt this way about anyone." I smiled and pulled my hair back into a ponytail.

We met back up with KK and Cory, who yelled, "Ready to get out of here."

"Sure, let's go. I like the sound of that," he replied as he grabbed my hand and we headed back to his ride.

Once we arrived back at his room, he stood in front of me and said, "I want this to go beyond forever."

Putting a smile on my face, I replied, "Me too."

He opened the door, and we walked in. He placed the "Do Not Disturb" sign outside the door.

We went to the bedroom and watched movies until we fell asleep. I had a good time with this man. I asked him why he was staying here and whether he had a home. He told me he had a three-story built for when he had children. He said he couldn't go back to his house because it reminded him of his deceased child. I apologized for prying and changed the subject.

We ordered in for the next few days. By the time we looked up, we had two days left. I wasn't ready to go back to Arkansas yet, but I had things to do, so I had no choice with or without KK.

He looked at me and asked what was on my mind. I told him nothing and kissed him. He gripped my body and pulled me over on top of him, and we kissed some more. He started fondling my breasts and removing all my clothes. I allowed everything to take place. As he kissed me all over my neck, he pulled my panties to the side. As I leaned back, he pulled out his manhood, and it stood straight up at attention.

I smiled and said, "Did I do that?"

He chuckled. "You always do that to me."

Loving the sound of that, I placed my essences on top and slowly eased my way down.

"Ooh," he moaned, and he grabbed me tightly, a little too tightly, if I may add, but I understood why.

"Damn, baby, you so tight!" he said.

"Is that a bad thing?" I asked.

"Hell, no," he answered with a weak sort of moan, letting me know I was doing a good thing to his body. I slowly ground his pole until he felt me cum all over his joystick. Over and over, I rode him as if this were my last time and my last night.

"Ah shit, girl, you're so damn good. How do you do that? How do you make me so weak?" he asked as he dragged every word slowly.

I didn't reply. I just gave him the best parts of me. He rolled me over so he could get on top. Laying me down, he pushed hard, and it went in smoothly as we both moaned on his entry. "I love you already," he whispered in my ear.

I didn't know how to respond, so I just moaned, "Yes," as he pleased me like never before. I felt my body temperature rise, and I became so hot from the motion we were creating.

"I feel you, baby. I feel you," I said, over and over. Moaning out un pure bliss so loudly. I guess that's when we both came.

We fell asleep in that exact position.

∼

Waking up in the middle of this Friday night, I felt funny, and I didn't know why. I felt as if someone was here in the room with me. But when I looked around, I saw no one.

He was sleeping and looked so peaceful that I didn't want to wake him. I swear I heard the chains on my purse jingle and a door closing. So, I got up and went into the front room to see if anyone was there. Not thinking to check my purse, I looked around.

As I walked to the light switch, I saw a body moving across the window outside. I hurried to open the door. I was too late. All I saw were two figures dressed in all black as the elevator doors closed. I called out for Tony real loud, and he jumped and ran to where I was. I told him what had happened, and he told me I was tripping. I knew better, so I asked if we could ask the front desk to see if they could check the cameras. Either that or I was out of here. After all, I had seen two people running for the already opened elevator.

Wanting me to feel better about staying with him, he agreed.

We talked to the night manager, and he agreed to the terms. To my surprise, someone *had* entered our room. He walked over to the front desk to see the ID of the visitor. It read "Lisa Brown." I asked who she was.

He answered, "My wife."

My heart dropped down to my feet. I walked away so upset, so heartbroken, saying to myself, *I knew he was too good to be true! This man sitting here with a whole wife on his team.* Hurt and confused, I walked to the door of the hotel and went outside for some air. At that moment everything was spinning. I became so upset with myself. I had fallen for a married man. Hell, I had slept with him.

I began to cry, walking down the sidewalk. He came up behind me grabbed my hand. I removed myself from his grip and proceeded to walk and cry. He walked around to my front and put his face on my face, holding me tightly so I couldn't get away.

"I said earlier when we first touched you were mine from this point on. I meant those words with every breath in me. I do not want to lose you over a woman who clearly does not want me."

"Doesn't look that way to me," I said. "She came in on us, and she wasn't alone, Tony! How could you not tell me she was your wife? Why did you feel the need to keep that from me? Was she the one who had your child?"

"Yes, she was also the one who asked for the divorce," he said.

"I thought we were on the same page," I said.

"We are. I want you. I choose you," he replied in a pleading voice.

"Just let me go. I need to think, Tony," I said as I tried to shake off his hand.

"I can't. They got away, and if I leave you alone, they might come back and see you walking."

"I can handle myself," I said as I pulled away again.

"Michelle, please, come back inside so we can talk," he said sadly.

Giving in, I returned to the hotel, and we talked on a sofa in the lobby. I hadn't realized I was so hurt. I really liked him. He explained everything: why they were living separately, how he had filed for divorce and she had signed it, how finalizing it was taking longer than expected.

Looking at him, I asked, "Do you feel it's safe to stay in that room?"

He told me he would get a room in my name if I wanted to so that way, I could feel safe. I told him he didn't have to; I could afford it myself. Up until, despite everything that had happened, he had not seemed upset. That is, until I told him I could afford to pay for the room myself.

"I didn't ask if you could," he said, "and I don't care that you can. I got it, and I'm getting it."

In a light tone, I asked, "Do I need to be afraid of you? You seem fine with her and whomever she was with, invading your privacy. But the moment I say I can handle paying for something, you get upset."

"As long as you are in my presence, it's my job, as a man, to take care of anything that you need. My dad taught me this when I was growing up and living under his roof. I see how well he treated my mother, and I want the same for my woman."

Allowing him to be the man he wanted to be, I went up with him to the sixteenth floor and entered the room. It was like his suite, but it was better than the twin queens KK and I had shared.

We went to sleep on top of the covers, and when the room was filled with sunlight, I opened my eyes to find myself alone. I dropped my head and said, "He is running to her aid right now."

After a while, I took a long shower and moped around in the bathrobe the hotel had provided. I wanted to text KK so badly, but I knew her time spent with Cory was coming to an end, and I didn't want to interrupt that. I had no clothes because I had left all my belongings inside Tony's suite. I found a channel with a good movie playing and just watched it.

The time was spilling into the middle of the day, and I had no other choice than to think of the worst-case scenario. He was with her, trying to please her and make her feel better about seeing me so that when I left, he could go home to her.

I wasn't about to get played by this man. I cursed myself for even giving him the chance to be with me, let alone feel the best parts of me. I shared those things with him because I thought he was the one.

I put on the gym shorts and T-shirt he had given me and headed for the door. I had it in mind to leave my truck keys, insurance card, and credit card at the front desk for KK to get back home while I grabbed a cab and took a flight back. I was all in my feelings. When I opened the door, there stood Tony with bags and bags of clothes.

"What is this?" I questioned.

He smiled and said, "I went shopping, and room service is on its way. I ordered us dinner. I wasn't gone too long, was I?" he asked in a slow voice, pausing after every word as he looked at my hands and noticed my little bag and purse.

"You were about to leave me?" he asked, looking confused. I had to explain my thoughts, so I told him what I had been thinking while he was gone.

He chuckled. "You are overthinking, baby girl. I will never just up and leave without telling you unless it's for a surprise. I wanted to do something for you to make up for my ex-wife's behavior."

"You do not have to shower me with gifts for someone else's actions. I don't blame you. And judging by the way you are treating me, I couldn't blame her if she still wanted you. You are a good man. Maybe she never noticed it until you were gone."

I had decided to be completely honest. He is a real man, and I am lucky I ran back into him.

"I'm still a little upset about you withholding the fact that you're still married. I feel like you will hold out on important things. It's hard for me to trust people once they do that."

He interrupted me, "I didn't keep it away. I just didn't want to run you away. You know how hard it is to find a good woman who is half a virgin and faithful to herself. Only to tell her, 'By the way, I'm married, but we are going through a divorce.' You would have run off, and I never would have seen you again. I am so sorry for keeping that away from you. I'm glad it's out now. I hope you understand and trust that I am in this for real. I need you, Michelle. I don't want to lose you. Not to her mistake. You are the kind of woman I need. She is not like you. She runs at the first sight of a problem. I need a stronger woman than her.

"I need you. I want you. I'm falling for you. I don't know why I'm having these feelings so soon. I just do. My mother always told me, "You will know the one when you see her." I understand that now. When I first saw you years back, my heart leaped. That same feeling came over me when I saw you this time around. I said to myself, *I can't let her get away this go-around.*" Looking down at me, he grabbed my face and kissed me.

There was a knock at the door.

"Ah, lunch is here," he said as he opened the door to the best-smelling salmon ever.

He was spoiling me, and I was getting used to it. He had also wiped away my doubts about him. He made me happy and always kept me smiling. I didn't want this to change for anything. I was falling for him deeply, and I didn't want to stop.

We enjoyed lunch and watched some TV. I was getting a little bored with the shows that were on, so I pulled out my phone and my portable speaker and played some slow jams. He grabbed my hand and pulled me into a slow dance.

"You are so much more fun than anyone I know," he complimented me, then turned me around to face the other side of the room. I could feel him smelling my hair. He kissed my head, then moved my hair to expose my neck.

Not knowing that is the most sensitive part of my body, he began to suck lightly on my neck. As he kissed down the center of my neck, chills sped across my body.

"I felt that," he said as he turned to kiss my lips. Your heartbeat is my heartbeat. I can keep you here forever."

"You know, I have to go home sometime," I said as he turned me back around to face the other direction.

"No, you don't. Forget that life and stay with me," he said in a low tone in my ear.

"I have to run my mother's cosmetic line. I have bills. I have their house to look after. I have a lot going on back home," I told him. "I can't just neglect my responsibilities."

He placed his head on the back of mine, pulled me closer to him, and whispered, "Please stay." I felt his hot breath on my neck, and I could tell he meant it. I turned to kiss him, and we locked lips for a long minute. Then we gazed into each other's eyes.

Breaking the silence, I said, "I have to drive KK back home, remember? I just can't leave her stranded. Why don't you come to me? Come back home with me so we can sort all this out," I asked.

"Okay, once you are back in Arkansas, call me and I'll book my flight." He picked up his phone and called someone to book a first-class flight to Little Rock. He then looked at me and said,

"Do not wait until you get to Little Rock to call. Call me once you are outside Texas."

"Okay," I said. We entertained each other some more, then we fell asleep.

When I awoke, I felt and heard my stomach growling.

"Someone's hungry, I hear?" I smiled and nodded. "Let's go out somewhere nice," he said.

I agreed and went to get fresh.

Dinner was satisfying. I think I overate by how stuffed I felt. We took another walk after we ate, but this time, it wasn't at the park with KK and Cory. We just walked around the hotel. I enjoyed this time with Tony, but I knew it was coming to an end. He was the best thing that had happened in Dallas. I didn't want to leave him, but I had to go. I told myself once we reach our hotel room that I was going to give him something to make him rush back to me. Once we settled in the bed that night, that is what I did.

The next morning, we slept until around four. We headed back up to his room, and that's when he told me he had changed rooms, ensuring no one could get in but me.

We shared a shower, and as the hot water fell onto our bodies, he began to wash me. He looked at me, and once my eyes locked with his, he kissed me tenderly and caressed the sides of my body. He traced his fingers across my hips and in between my inner thighs. He then touched my love nest, making me moan softly in his ear. He picked me up and pinned me against the shower wall. As he eased his shaft inside me, slowly grinding it in me, I melted on top of it. Things got pretty wild as he long-stroked me up against the wall. I squeezed my legs around him so tightly, loving how he made me feel. Our bodies had gotten weak, and we both released. Placing me back onto my feet, he washed off my body, and I washed his. He then oiled my body oil down while helping me put on my sundress.

He asked, "Can you leave the clothes that's already here in the closet next to mine?"

I smiled and felt a little special that moment. "Yes," I said.

We cuddled on the sofa until KK and Cory called, saying they were on the way so we could head out.

"Now, promise me you are going to call me when you touch Arkansas grounds. I want to know you made it home safely before I show up not knowing where to go. Once I touch down, I will call you to pick me up from the airport. Is that cool with you?" he asked.

"Yes, anything for you, baby," I replied with a kiss. He picked me up, leaned me against the wall, and said, "You feel that?"

My heart skipped beats, and I replied, "Yes."

He said, looking me deep in my eyes, "That is all mine, and you can't share this feeling with no one else but me."

"I understand, this is all yours and only yours," I said as I kissed the tip of his nose.

He then went in under my dress and said, "This here belongs to me. I am a very stingy man."

Bursting into laughter, we kissed and made our way to the door. We walked down to my truck and started loading all the things I had collected during my stay. That's when KK and Cory pulled up next to us. We all said our goodbyes, and we headed off.

"I really enjoyed myself," I told KK.

"Thanks for changing our plans from Atlanta to Dallas. It was the best move you ever made," I said, smiling and feeling good. Waving goodbye, we headed for the highway.

CHAPTER 18

Breaking Down

Drake

All motherfucking week and all weekend this girl have been gone! No call, no text, no damn letter for that matter! I do not know what the fuck she is thinking, but she better get her motherfucking mind right! You don't pull this shit on me! Does she not know who the fuck I am? She better not has been with any motherfucking man at that! I was thinking and pacing the floor thinking about my girl and where in the fuck she could be.

"Fuck!" I yelled, punching my punching bag as hard as I could. I'd been lifting weights and running all week to keep my cool. Here it was, Sunday again, and she had not arrived home. I knew I knew better than to leave her ass there. I just thought she was going to beat me home and change the locks. I didn't want to be locked out of my own home this time around, so I tried to beat her home.

The dumbest move I could have made.

Oooh! If this girl been with someone else, I am going to kill her! I thought, but then I changed my mind. I loved her too much to kill her, but I would have been so hurt if she did. I stopped myself in mid-thought. *She not that type of woman, so*

I have no worries. I just need to chill and calm my nerves. She just very upset with me—that's all.

Looking at my phone to see if she called or text, I got nothing, and that nothing was hurting me and pissing me off at the same damn time. All I know was I had to get out of this house. I went by her mothers to talk to her and see if she had seen or heard from KK. When I got there, she was nice and sweet. She made me a sandwich and asked what I had done. I knew I shouldn't tell her, but at this time, I needed her to understand. I told her that KK had found me in a hotel with Amanda—and that I had the same type of relationship with Kerry that I had with Amanda. I met them both a week apart, and I had been with both ever since. After I told her the story, she said, "You know Amanda blames Kerry for her twin brother's death. She had a run-in with her twin brother's friend Brad. Kerry told Brad that Amanda would be a better choice for her. Then Kerry started seeing Allen."

I told her I had found that out after KK left me in the room with Amanda. I asked, "Is that the reason she hasn't come home?" I told her I was worried about her, and I asked her for her daughter's hand in marriage. I told her about the three dozen roses I had ordered, placing them all over the living room along with a 3-carat diamond ring to ask her to marry me. When I left KK's mother's house, I felt a little better, but I still missed my girl. Still not at ease, I went running through our neighborhood to clear my head and kill some time. I was still uneased and worried, so I broke down and called my mother. I knew she would have the answer.

"Hello, baby. Long time since you called me. How are you doing?" she asked.

"I'm doing okay, Momma," I said.

"Now, baby, Momma knows when something is upsetting her baby. Want to tell me the truth this time?"

I didn't know how she knew, but she knew. I couldn't lie to my mom, so I told her everything—everything I had told Kerry's mom. Once I finished telling her the story, all that sweet talk about Momma's baby went out the window.

"I wouldn't come home either if I had found your daddy red-handed. You could have told her how you felt and half the truth, but she caught you in the act. Now, tell me something, Drake, if it was her you found in the bed half-nude with another man, what would you have done?"

Hurt by the question itself, I said, "Leave her."

She replied, "My point exactly. You knew better than that to be with that other woman. I thought I raised you better than that. I promise, you are just like your father when he was young and dumb." She said in her angry tone, "Now get off my phone and go find a way to make it up to your woman. She doesn't deserve that from you."

"Yes, ma'am," I said before we hung up. *I should have known better,* I said to myself.

All I could do was wait and wait and wait. I missed my girl, and she was gone—for how long, I didn't know. I just had to wait.

I kept myself busy so I wouldn't drive myself crazy. I was overwhelmed with thoughts of what she was doing and thinking of how badly I had hurt her. I got out of the house to keep from thinking of her. I loved her, and the last thing I wanted to do was hurt her.

I went to the park to ball with my boys. The whole gang was here, like old times. When they saw me, suddenly, they were getting crunk, hyping me up and shit. I heard one of my boy's yell, "Oh, shit, it's about to get real."

I took my shirt off and threw it against the fence. My boy threw me the ball, and it was on from there. I mean, we balled for hours, and at some point, I thought about KK, but I was so busy trying to win. I tried to dunk hard on this win and landed hard on my back. After that, I was ready to go. Couldn't play anymore.

I felt like that fall was some form of punishment for what I had done. I got inside my car and sat there for a while, thinking of what I could do to keep my mind off her.

After I got home, I showered, then passed out.

I took myself to the movies the next day, thinking about KK. I went to work all week and even took on some extra shifts. I worked my volunteer job both weekends.

Today is Sunday, and I have not heard from this girl.

I got so upset I punched a hole in the wall. Now I'm trying to YouTube how to patch it up before she comes home. If she comes home, hell, I guess it's over between us. Might as well do something to make me feel better. I grabbed my phone and started flipping through my contact list.

I came to Candace's name.

"Hello."

"What's up, girl? What are you doing?" I asked.

"What do you want?" she asked with attitude.

"Can I come over? I need to relieve some stress," I said, sounding all masculine, grabbing on my manhood.

"Come by and I'll see what I can do," she replied, then she hung up. *Always straight to the point with her sassy ass*, I thought. I showered and headed to her.

When I arrived, she had just made dinner. She made me a big-ass plate, then she fetched me a beer. We talked throughout the meal about what we were going to do about the booty calls.

She knew I had KK, so I didn't know why she was asking that shit. I just played it off to get what I wanted, like always.

It wasn't until she kissed me that I realized I didn't want her. I didn't want this thing we had going. I just wanted to go home.

I told her I had to use her bathroom. Dodging this bullet, I left.

I needed my girl. I needed KK. At this point, all I wanted to do was apologize for my wrongdoing. I needed her to know how bad I felt.

I just wanted her forgiveness. If she was this mad not to come home, then she really was done with me. I had to accept it and move on. Until then, I had to tell her I was sorry.

I walked to the bedroom for a pillow to lay on the sofa and wait to see if she came home tonight. It smelled just like her. She had me so weak.

I took a shot, then another one. I found a movie, then I fell asleep.

I never knew how much I needed this girl until she wasn't here. She must come home sooner or later.

CHAPTER 19

She Is Fucking with the Wrong Man

Lisa A. Brown

When I was about to give birth to my baby, we were one happy family. Tony was a good man, a gentleman, a hardworking man, and now he was about to be a family man. A daddy for the first time, and I was going to be a mother for the first time. Our home was happy, and our love was faithful.

We met back in college our first year. He was the nicest guy I had ever met. He treated me like a lady in every way. He would walk me to class, and we would go to the library and study together. Or he would pop in just to surprise me with Starbucks. We encouraged each other when we needed lifting. We were a real team and good support system.

We married a year after we moved into our first apartment off campus. He introduced me to Amanda, and we became close friends. She was a sweet girl when I met her. She was always by herself when I saw her. She had friends; it just always seemed like she was missing someone. She was closed off, but I brought her out of her shell. She hung with me and began to make friends. One day, I asked her why she was so standoffish. That's when I found out she had a twin who died. I felt bad for her, and I grew to her like the sister I never had. I was trying to make up for the brother she had lost.

She was with his cousin Cory. I used to think they were brothers because of how close they were. But it was their dads who were brothers. I have been in their family for four years, and boy, did they teach me the value of family, relationships, and marriage. He was raised by good, hardworking, wealthy people. I, on the other hand, was running from my mother's boyfriend. He would get drunk and beat me, and sometimes my mother too if she tried to stop him.

I couldn't wait to get out of that house. He paid all the bills, so that was one of the reasons she acted as if she couldn't leave him. My dad wasn't a good man, but he didn't beat on us. He was never home because he was a drug dealer. She had to drop out of school to take care of me. I think she regrets me at times.

My little sister, on the other hand, was treated like royalty. She was his only child, so he favored her over my mother and me. He was a city worker, so he made pretty good money. There were moments when he would be nice. But when he got drunk, the beatings would come.

I felt helpless and motherless at times. I used to think it was my looks that made him not like me. I took after my father—full lips, milk chocolate skin. I put you in the mind of Naomi Campbell, the model. I just wasn't as tall. My mother and sister were light skinned. It was hard for me to make friends in middle and high school, so I made a very good friend out of the school's counselors. They would listen to me when I needed someone to talk to. They also helped me rebuild my self-esteem. I never told them about my stepdad hitting me; otherwise, they would have had me removed from the home.

But when I got to college and met Tony, he was the best thing that ever happened. I didn't like him or want him at first, but when I saw how rich he was, I decided the love would come.

I already had a boyfriend, and he was a bad guy, a gang member who kept me with money if I slept with him. He was sneaky and observant when it came to matters of money. He claimed he loved me, but I knew better. He would down me also for my hair not being real and how my breasts wasn't big enough. I used to think he was the man of my dreams, how he would come and rescue me from my mean ass stepdad. Wanting to forget about him, I lied and told Tony he was my first after my ex went to prison for twenty-five years. He was convicted of a home robbery invasion. He was identified as the main and only suspect.

That was another good thing that happened for me. I was a nurse, and I had an in-home care patient. He sort of lost it after his wife died. I showed Orlando how to rob my patient without getting caught. I got out of that for free. That is, until he took the whole charge without ratting me out. I used to write him from time to time, but once my feelings were gone, the letters stopped.

I was happy once Tony and I started living together. He showered me with his money, and he was a real gentleman. I guess a part of me knew he was good, so I stayed with him. When we got married, he allowed me to plan the biggest wedding a girl could dream of. I invited my mother and her boyfriend to my wedding, but they didn't show. I think it was because their precious child whom they shared was in a bad domestic relationship. They didn't want to be happy for me because he felt bad for treating me the way he did. Karma came to bite him in his ass with his own child. I reached out to help my sister, but she was too much like Momma, so she felt like he loved her since he beat her. Apple didn't fall too far, huh?

Enough about them and back to us.

We honeymooned in Cancun, Mexico. That was the best time of my life. We came home and finished college a year apart. He attended my graduation, and I attended his. We were the perfect couple, said everyone. He would have gone on to go play pro football, but his dad wanted a businessman for their company.

He owns a handful of franchises. He is the CEO of the biggest arena here in Texas. He doesn't brag on his success much because money has always been in their family. When I met his mother, she would always tell me to allow her son to be the man in the relationship. She loved the fact that I had my degree in technology; she just didn't want me to outshine my husband. She was a very nice woman, but I could tell there was some 'hood in her. She had that don't-cross-me look about her. So, I stayed in her good graces.

His dad was totally different—laid-back, cool, funny guy. He was proud of his son taking after him. He used to ask for grandkids. When I got pregnant, I couldn't wait to tell them. I knew that would have made their world brighter. Tony was an only child, so they were itching for a baby.

Joy filled my heart. I didn't tell my mother because I didn't want her or her boyfriend to have the chance to hurt my child the same way they'd hurt me.

We build a nursery and painted it pink, yellow, and purple. I already knew she would be beautiful and kind, just like her parents. We were going to name her Mona Lisa Brown, after his mother, Ramona, and myself. The love I felt for my unborn child was undeniable.

Tony would come in from work and talk to her for hours through my belly. He always had his hands on my stomach, kissing and talking. I loved it. When she got a few months older, she would kick at the sound of her dad. I knew then she was a daddy's girl. It was beautiful and amazing how my life turned around and how good things had gotten. Tony was the best thing that ever happened to me.

When it was time to have the baby, I was making me a bowl of ice cream. I felt something warm and wet running down my thighs. Now, when you are pregnant, things change for you. Like peeing, for instance. If I laughed or coughed hard, I peed a little. So, when I rubbed my hand on my legs with the paper towel, expecting it to be yellow, I was surprised to find it was blood red. My mouth dropped, and I gasped for air. Noticing how big the puddle was, I panicked, holding on to the kitchen counter so I wouldn't slip.

I made my way upstairs to call Tony for help. He told me to grab the emergency bags we had prepared. Then he told me to make my way to unlock the door. He said he was sending Amanda to me, as he was boarding a flight to be on his way here. Amanda made it to me in no time. She rushed to get into the car, and on our way there, she rounded up all the family for Tony and me.

Once we made it to the hospital and I was being wheeled back to be set up, Tony called, telling me he loved me and that he wished he were here. The pain I was bearing had me angry that he wasn't here now, when I needed him. Instead, he was on his way to the hospital from a business trip in New York.

When she came, she wasn't breathing. The doctors did everything they could to save her. It just wasn't enough. This labor I endured was the hardest thing in my life. So, when Tony arrived, I had already told the doctor not to let anyone else see her.

I was so hurt and full of bitterness. I couldn't find the words to tell them all to leave. I was so hurt by Tony that I had no feeling after I lost Mona Lisa Brown.

I was rushed to the hospital by Amanda because she picked the fine time to come early. Tony was out of town, and by the time he made it, it was already too late.

I told him the night before not to go, that I had a feeling she was on her way. If she had heard her daddy's voice, she would have made it. I knew she would have. Once we came home, we just sat in silence. He was good to me, I will admit. He made sure I was comfortable. He would cry in the nursery late at night so I wouldn't hear or see him. That made me mad as hell. I felt like he was hiding his emotions from me. I would cry all over the place. Not him; he went to her room and let go without me.

Which probably was the right thing to do since I blamed him in front of his family for not being there. They all turned a cold shoulder to me, even Cory. He stopped coming by the house with Amanda and all. He even told Amanda not to be my friend anymore, but she would sneak to come see me.

One day, when they had a bad misunderstanding about some cheerleader, she came to see me, and he followed her. He told her right in front of me that he didn't want her anymore. She was already hurt by him cheating, but he found out about her coming over. That's what broke them up. He told her she couldn't be trusted because she still hung around me after he told her not to. Her being around me was the icing on the cake.

As if I'm such a horrible person. Anyway, back to us again. He did things without me, and that made me furious at him. I went on a rampage of anger and accused him of being with someone else, choosing his job over the baby and me. I blamed him and took it all out on him. I even yelled for a divorce, and that sent him away. I guess I thought he would be there no matter what.

A month later, he tricked me. He asked me to sign papers in case something happened to him. They turned out to be prenuptial agreement papers. On top of divorce, he really took me seriously when I ask for the divorce. I don't get a thing out of this but what I came in with. He thinks he can just throw me away after all this? No! I don't think so. I was there with him. I lost my child too. Now he all happy with this bitch, and I won't have it.

I walked into his suite, and I saw the two of them asleep. I stole her ID and credit card and used it to rent a car while my cousin drove his car back to her house and waited for her ass to get here. I chose to have my cousin with me so I wouldn't be alone. He was going to help me get rid of her ass. If I can't have him, no one can.

So, now I am here in the back of her house while I wait for my cousin to break in so we can sit and wait for her to show up.

Once he was in, he motioned for me to come in. This bitch had it made. She didn't need Tony for his money. She had money as well, so the fact she didn't have an alarm on her house was the stupidest thing. As we went through her things, Pat, my cousin—who, by the way, is as gay as they come—was stealing her name-brand clothes that still had tags on them.

He was too big for her small and very short frame, so he stole it for his tiny-ass boyfriend. He loaded up all her shit in that rental that we got off her credit card. Yes, I know I sound like a totally different person from Tony's wife, but this woman was taking the very thing I had worked hard to fall in love with and keep. I see why she had so many rings, bracelets, and diamond necklaces. I took some of that shit too, even the one she had sitting all alone in a jewelry case. We went through every inch of her two-story home. Why so much space for one person, I don't know. We found a safe in her bedroom, but we couldn't get it opened, and it was too heavy for us to take. Boy, did we want it, though. Lucky ass, this homewrecker had a lot going for herself. She had expensive makeup by the cases, like was she the owner of this famous cosmetic line or something. The little whore had it made for real. I went through her house from top to bottom. My cousin Pat broke a window out from her basement door.

I'm still not understanding why she didn't have an alarm. All these luxury clothes and furniture she had was enough to make one rich. I had to put a stop to her. She had enough money to buy her own man, so I don't know why she chose to mess with mine.

We waited for hours for this woman to pull into her driveway. We did our car a few blocks over and just waited. We ate her food and drank her expensive-ass bottles of wine. We hid in a room that looked like her office, in the closet. We waited on her to show up, and while we waited, we talked about how we were going to let it all go down.

Pat didn't like her once he seen how rich, smart, and beautiful she was. I think it's in a gay man nature to be intimidated by a beautiful woman. He had something smart to say about her every time he seen a beautiful photo of her. I didn't care how good she looked; she couldn't have my man. That was the only reason I was here.

We talked out our plan: Pat was going to grab her, tie her up, and blindfold her. I was going to threaten her life if she didn't stop seeing Tony. That's all. Nothing too harmful. If she knew better, maybe she would do better. It seemed like forever, so we went into her kitchen to find something else to eat.

That's when we heard her walking in. We hid while Pat snuck around a door. As she approached the hallway to where she could almost see me, Pat grabbed her from behind and placed a pillowcase over her face. Somehow, she got free from him. She hit him in the face with her elbow, knocking his gold tooth out his mouth. I must say, that was a really bad move, a real no-no.

He went crazy and beat her as if she were a man, throwing her from wall to wall, slamming her to the ground, and beating her all over her body and face. I really didn't care to much for her since she was stealing my man. So, I let him do it. He beat her so bad, it brought flashbacks of my stepdad beating me. That is what made me stop him.

By then, it was too late. She was motionless on the floor. We left her house in a hurry, leaving her front door wide open and without a trace of evidence, since we had gloves on the whole time. I saw a different side of my cousin Pat as we made it to the car. His jealousy was over-the-top hate, and it had me a little shaken. I didn't want her dead, and we were so scared of getting caught.

I asked him why he had changed the plan. He said because she hit him in his face and got away, and he don't play that shit about his face. We threw out her credit card and hurried back to his car to ditch the rental so there was no way we could get caught. Everything we did was over the phone and through her name. we drove out of Arkansas in a hurry. I was relieved once we reached Texas and found his boyfriend. After we showered him with some of the makeup and all the clothes he could fit into, we asked could this cover for his help. And could we use him as an alibi for the crime we had just committed.

His happy gay ass said yes with a smile on his face if I would agree to give him the diamond necklace I stole from her ass. I let him have it. Shit, I wanted to pawn it for what it was worth. I told Pat to sell all the rest of the stuff and split the money down the middle and get lost.

I went to a bar near my house for a drink to unwind my mind. I hated what Pat had done to her, but I was hoping she would get the picture and leave my man alone. I had a few too many drinks, and it took my mind off the dramatic episode. Well, now that that was over, I went home to our big three-story house, which Tony allowed me to keep once the divorce was final.

I know what I did was wrong, but I wasn't ready to end my marriage with Tony. It wasn't finalized, so I still had time to win him back. I thought if I eliminated her, he would get over it and come home to me.

All I can do now was wait and see what time has to offer. I just hope he doesn't find another woman and forget about me. We have been through too much just to walk away. Hell, we have a bond, and we share the loss of our child. I do love him, and I will do anything to get him back. Anything!

CHAPTER 20

On Our Way Home

Kerry

Michelle called me early Sunday morning to make sure we were up. Today, we were leaving to head back to Arkansas. We party so hard last night, I asked her if we could stay a few more hours, but she said no. Michelle wanted to get a head start on the road, so we'd have enough time to relax and get ourselves ready for work Monday.

She told me she would drive the whole way home so I could get some rest. She knew I'd been clubbing the whole weekend with Cory. She and Tony just sat in their hotel suite all weekend, cuddling and getting to know each other.

"Bae wake up. We gotta go."

"I'm not ready for you to leave," he said in a sleepy voice.

"I don't want to leave either, but Michelle is ready, and I don't want her fussing at me."

"Turnover, baby girl."

"What?"

"I want to taste your love once more before you leave me here by my lonesome," he said as he started to tug at my thong. "Take your damn panties off and sit on my face," he said with his eyes still closed because he wasn't ready to get up. "I'm dead serious, Kerry. I want to taste you before you leave."

"Well, turn over on your back and wake the fuck up."

"I am awake. I'm just waiting on you to bring your ass over here."

"Cory, for real, we can't do this right now."

I got on up and had Cory drop me off at the hotel. Before we got there, he stopped at a donut shop and got everyone a breakfast sandwich with a donut. *This man is so sweet and thoughtful,* I thought. I could tell he didn't want me to leave. He held my hand the whole ride to Michelle's. He told me to think about this week and to call him as often as I could every day so he could hear my voice. He'd have his phone on him and would answer no matter what time it was. I just looked at him and smiled. I think he could tell I wasn't ready to go either, since I was quiet most of the ride.

There was something about this man that had me head over hills. Like, it has only been nine days, and already I was hooked.

Once we pulled up the front of the hotel, Cory got out to open my door, then went to the back to grab my bags. We walked to Michelle's truck, and he placed my bags in the back seat, and then he came to the front where I was to hug and kiss me.

"Whenever you're ready to come back, my door is always open for you, beautiful."

"Thank you so much for this weekend. You saved me from a lot of tears, and I enjoyed myself the whole time I was here. There was not one dull moment," I said, hugging him back.

"All right then, Kerry," Tony said as he closed Michelle's door. "Be careful, ladies."

"I hope to see you soon," Cory said as I put on my seatbelt.

"Bae, I will call you every day and we will talk."

"I'm looking forward to it," he said as he closed the door.

I looked over at Michelle and told her, "Cory is so amazing." I smiled and closed my eyes, soaking in all our fun times. He was a breath of fresh air compared to Drake.

I could have stayed another week. She was glad I had enjoyed myself but then spilled the beans on what went down these last couple days with her. That wasn't what I was expecting to hear. The last two days had been a mess, and it made me feel some type of way, because I didn't know all this stuff with Tony's soon-to-be ex-wife was going down. Threw me for a loop to know all this was taking place while I was out enjoying being single for my birthday.

I just wanted to see my friend happy. Tony might still be the one for her, but he had to put this bitch in her place.

We spent the rest of the ride talking about what we did each day and going into details. We were just smiling and laughing at each other 'cause this weekend had started out lame. I mean, we hit up the clubs, but the guys brought life into it. We never thought it would turn out this way, and for the both of us, finding people we really liked who we already knew. What are the odds of that?

We made it back to Elle's house. I got into my car and made sure Elle made it inside. We decided we'd separate the bags later, since there were so many from our shopping trips. Once I saw her go inside, I pulled off and headed home to pack. When I pulled into the driveway, Drake's car was parked there.

Damn, he here, I thought. *I don't feel like this shit. I'm tired and hungry.*

As soon as I walked to the door and reached for the knob, Drake opened the door.

"Baby, I'm sorry."

Damn, I thought, *can I walk in the house first?*

"Where you been?"

"I been in Texas, Drake."

"All this time?"

"Um … yeah," I said, rolling my eyes.

"I know you seen me calling you. Why you didn't answer?"

"Really, Drake, you really gon' ask me that stupid question like you don't already know. I didn't want to hear shit you had to say, and I still don't want to hear it."

"Please, Kerry, do you want me to get on my knees and beg you." Drake got on his knees and put his hands together like he was praying.

"Why you asking me? Did you ask me if I wanted you to cheat on me?"

"Kerry!"

I threw my hands up like, "Boy, bye."

"Kerry!"

"Drake, say what the fuck you gotta say!"

"Damn, you mean!" he said, dragging his words.

"Well, I wasn't like this before I left, was I?"

"Baby, I love you. I want to be with you. You see, I bought all these roses for you," he said, walking toward the dead roses, grabbing a little black box.

Drake walked toward me with the little black box and got on his knees again.

"I know I hurt you, Kerry, but seeing how I hurt you hurt me, and I don't never want to see you like this again. I promise, I will make you happy, and I will never cheat on you again. Will you marry me?"

"No. Just because you ask me to marry you doesn't mean I'm supposed to forgive, and I'm damn sure not going to forget."

"Kerry, I'm not letting you leave here. I don't want to be without you."

"Oh my God!" I said, frustrated. "If the shoe was on the other foot, would you have forgiven me? Oh, and your ass hasn't been trying to marry me, but now that I caught your ass suddenly, you want to marry me? No, Drake, 'cause the shit isn't real. This the second time you messed around on my birthday."

"But, Kerry," he said, interrupting me.

"Kerry my ass. You fucked up, Drake. Now deal with it."

My phone started ringing in my hand. When I turned it over, I smiled wide? It was Cory calling. I hit the ignore button.

"Damn, you were just fussing at me. Now you're smiling. Who the hell was that?"

"A friend."

"Kerry, two wrongs don't make it right."

"You know what, Drake? You're right. But it'll make me feel better."

My phone rang again, so I hit the ignore button again. *Ding* went the sound, letting me know I had a voice message.

"Damn, see what that nigga wants!"

"I know what he wants, Drake!"

"And what's that?"

"Me!"

As I walked toward the hall, I noticed a hole in the wall.

"What the hell happen here?" I asked.

When Drake turned his head, I hurried and put my phone on silent. I hated to do Cory like that, but I didn't want to hear Drake's mouth. I'd call him as soon as I left.

"I got mad at myself for what I done to you and took it out on the wall."

"But you got a punching bag in the other room, so why you are punching holes in my wall?"

"I was punching that too, but at the time I got mad, the wall was right there, and I wasn't thinking. So why the hell your phone lighting up? You put it on silent, didn't you, trying to be sneaky with the shit. That's probably why you wanted to take your ass to Texas."

"Hold up. Don't try to flip the script on me. I met him while I was in Texas, after I caught you and Amanda together."

"Really, really, Kerry? So, you just meeting random guys, giving them your number just because you mad at me. That's stupid, Kerry. What if he tried to do something to you?"

"Since you know so fucking much Drake, he's an old friend I met back when I was in school. That bitch Amanda know who he is because they used to talk, but I don't know if they kept in touch. It's kind of funny how we all were in Texas together. You weren't even supposed to be there. You, the one being sneaky and shit so you can have that bitch. She isn't nothing but a hoe, and you fell in line just like the rest of those lowlifes."

"Fuck that bitch!"

"You already did that!" I yelled, walking into the bedroom, grabbing clothes out of the closet and laying them on the bed.

"Whoa … wait a minute. What the hell you doing? You just going to move out like that?"

I didn't say anything. I just kept going to the closet, grabbing more clothes and shoes. I just walked past him, not looking him in his face. I went there with one thing on my mind, and that was to get my belongings. Drake walked out of the room and went to sit on the couch. I looked over at my phone and saw I had a text message. I forgot Cory was calling me. I went into the bathroom, locked the door, and called Cory. He said it was an emergency.

"Kerry."

"Cory, I'm so sorry."

"I thought something had happened to you."

"No, baby, I'm fine. I—"

He cut me off.

"Tony is at the airport waiting on Michelle, but she won't answer the phone. All this time, I been calling you was to see if you heard from her and why she had my family flying there if she didn't really want him there."

"Hold up. She do want him here. Let me call her to see what's going on."

I hung up the phone with Cory and dialed Elle's phone. It just rang. I hung up and called again, but no answer. She only lived ten minutes away, so I'd just jump in the car and run over there. I'd just left her. Maybe she fell asleep and just didn't hear her phone ringing. I grabbed my purse and ran to the front door.

"Where are you going?" Drake said.

I ignored him and kept going out the door.

"Kerry!" Drake said as he ran to the door and yelled.

"I gotta go check on Michelle!"

When I got in the car, I dialed Elle's number again. My Bluetooth picked up and put the phone through the speaker. No answer. I burned rubber as I pulled out of the driveway. Drake just stood there, puzzled. He didn't know what was going on.

As I got closer to her house, I saw flashing blue lights. It was so bright I had to put down the sun visor. *What the hell is going on?* I thought. I couldn't tell whose house they were at until I got closer and saw men walking around her yard and in and outside her house. I stopped my car in the middle of the street and jumped out.

"What happened?" I yelled. "Where's Michelle?"

"I think something bad has happened to your friend!" Mrs. Johnson said, standing in her yard, looking over at Elle's house wearing her robe and rollers in her head. It looked like Mrs. Johnson had been crying.

Mrs. Johnson was Elle's neighbor. She was in her late seventies, was a widow, and had about eight cats living with her. She was always outside when I went to Elle's house, so she was familiar with my face. She was a nosey little elderly white lady. She would come outside and go straight to her flowerbed when she heard us outside standing around talking and laughing.

I ran through the yard as news reporters tried to step in my path, but I ran right past them.

"Ma'am, can we talk to you for a minute?"

I ignored them and ran to the house. Once I made it into the doorway, I stopped, and my mouth dropped. I couldn't believe my eyes. Michelle's furniture was turned upside down. There was blood on the carpet and on the lampshade. Her TV had been torn from the wall. It looked like a tornado ran through it.

"Michelle ... Michelle," I yelled, walking from the living room to the kitchen and back into the living room. I was expecting to see my friend scared and wrapped in a blanket, talking to the officers. Oh, but this was not the case at all.

"Oh, excuse me."

"Ma'am, who are you? Please have a seat so you can calm down and talk."

"I'm Michelle's best friend, Kerry. We got back from Texas not too long ago. I watched her go inside the house as I pulled off. So, what happened here? Why do it look like someone came in here and robbed her?"

"Well, not only did she get robbed, but they beat her."

"What? Where is she?"

"The ambulance took her to the UAMS hospital. The neighbor realized her door was wide open for a long time and knew that was unusual, so she called the police. Once we got here, we found her in here in the hallway, lying in a puddle of blood, unresponsive."

"Oh my God!" I said with tears running down my face.

"Kerry, right?"

"Yes!"

"Did Michelle have a boyfriend, or was she involved with a guy?"

"No. She been single for a while. I would know. She's my best friend."

"Do you know if she was into it with anyone? Did anyone want to hurt her?"

"No," I said as my phone started ringing. It was Cory, so I answered.

"Hello!"

"Hey, what's up? Did you ever hear from your girl?"

"Cory, someone robbed and beat her bad!"

"Who?"

"Michelle."

"What!"

"Yes, she's at the hospital. I'm here, at her house ..." I paused a bit, overcome by sadness. "Talking to the detective. I'll call you back." I hung up without him saying a word. "Look, sir, I gotta go to the hospital and check on my friend," I said, rushing out the door not giving him a chance to say anything.

I slowed down once I got in the hallway. There were blood stains on the wall where Michelle might have tried to stand up but fallen back down. Lamps was knocked over. I even saw some of her portraits all broken up. This was crazy. How could ... why would someone want to hurt her? All kinds of things were running through my head. I'd never seen anything like this.

As I made it back outside, the crowd had died down, and people were walking back to their houses. Reporters was packing up their equipment, placing them in the van. One still tried to rush over to me.

"Ma'am, my name is Brooklyn from *Channel 7 News*. May I please ask you some questions?"

"Look, lady. My friend is in the hospital, and I don't know if she alive or fighting for her life. Please show some respect and get out my face with that."

"I'm sorry, ma'am. I'm just doing my job. I hope your friend is all right. Your friend is Michelle Dream, right?"

"Yes."

"She's a very popular person with her family history of cosmetics, so I'm sure the public would like an update."

"We'll see," I said as I got in my car in pulled off.

My phone started ringing. It was Drake.

"Hello!"

"Baby, is everything all right?"

"No, Drake. Someone hurt Michelle, and now she's in the hospital. I'm not coming back tonight, so don't wait up."

"Where is she?"

"UAMS."

"I'm coming up there!"

"No, Drake!"

Before I had a chance to continue, he hung up.

It All Happened So Fast

Tony

My baby just called and let me know she was back inside the limits of her state. She sounded so sexy over the phone, I missed her already. After I hung up, I called the airport to set out for the next flight to Little Rock. I had four hours to pack and had to be there before my plane boarded. I called Cory to let him know I was heading out to see Michelle.

He told me to be safe and have fun and to call if I needed a ride when I came back. I told him I had paid for security parking at the airport, so I was cool. I sat down in first class and made sure I was sitting alone because I brought the office on the go with me. Yes, I had to bring work to make sure bills got paid.

She knew I was bringing work, and I knew she was going to have to work as well. I didn't know exactly what she did for a living, but it didn't matter. I was just happy to be with my baby. I had a few drinks to settle my nerves for the flight. I ate a good meal because I didn't want to burden her with my hunger once I got to her.

Putting everything on hold was what I really wanted to do. I was falling for this woman, and I knew I needed to tell my folks before I made anything permanent. Really, though, it was already permanent. I was falling in love with this woman. I couldn't stop myself if I wanted to. I was chasing her by being on my way to Arkansas. The week went by too fast, and there weren't enough hours in a day. I'd never met any woman like her before in my life.

She was amazing and beautiful, inside and out, soft and sensual. I needed her in my life, and I wasn't about to give any other guy the opportunity to have what was mine.

With an hour to kill before my flight, I pulled out my phone and called my mother.

"Hello, Tony! Why are you calling this late in the evening?"

"Hey, Mom. How are you and Dad?" I asked.

"We are good, hon. What's wrong?" she said, noticing it was a little after 4 p.m. Normally when I call my parents, it's early in the morning, right before lunch.

"Nothing much. Just wanted to tell you and Dad I met a woman."

"Did you, my dear? Is she with you now?" she asked.

"No, ma'am."

"So, tell me about her," my mother said eagerly.

"Do you remember when we came home for spring break my first year in college?" I asked.

"Yes, the year Cory had your uncle's yacht. Had me worried sick. Yes, what about it?"

"Well, I ran back into the girl you saw in the picture I took with Cory and Amanda, her twin brother, and Kerry."

"Oh, you did, huh? I see. So where?" my mother asked, being nosey.

"At the bar lounge inside the hotel where I'm staying. She was sitting all alone, and I thought she was with her husband or boyfriend or waiting on her date. When I saw her, my heart skipped a beat?"

"Really!" she said, interrupting me.

"Yes," I said with a giggle. "I didn't know it was her until I approached her. She didn't notice me until I told her who I was. She was happy after I told her. I asked was she waiting on someone? She said no. Then she went on to say she was in town with her best friend. Which is the other young lady in the photo. It was the other young lady's birthday. We went on to talk about how our lives had been since we left off."

"Seems you two really hit it off," my mother said.

"We did, Momma. She ended up staying the full week with me. I enjoyed myself with her. I asked her to stay longer, but she said she had a business to run, bills to pay, and her mother and father's house to maintain."

"Sounds like a busy woman. She has any kids?" my mom questioned.

"That's the thing, Momma. she had only been with one guy one time. She said she was in love with him until she found out he sold drugs. He's doing federal time now. She said that broke her heart and made it hard for her to trust. I had doubts about her, until we went out for her friend's birthday at Cory's club. Her friend got a little drunk and said she needed a man. She put it out there that she was a virgin," I said, laughing. "It embarrassed her, but I told her she had nothing to be ashamed of."

My mother started laughing. "When do we get to meet this woman, Tony?"

I told her that I was on my way to Arkansas to visit her and get to know her better before I got my hopes up and brought her to meet my parents.

"I don't want her to be another disappointment to you and Dad, like Lisa was. Speaking of Lisa," I said, "did you know she came to my suite unannounced in the middle of the night? She walked in on us. We were sleeping when Michelle woke up and caught her leaving. She ran so fast, by the time I came to the door, she was gone."

"Tony, please do not have that young lady in the middle of you and Lisa's mess. That will run a woman away really quick," Momma said.

"Yes, ma'am," I replied before we said our goodbyes. She told me to have a safe trip and call her when I landed and when I returned home.

Lisa was a good woman when I met her. She was sweet and shy because of the abuse had she endured in her life. She was outgoing once I got to know her. We were very much in love and inseparable. We did everything together, went everywhere together.

My family took her in once we learned about her past. My mother knew better, though. She would always say, "It's something about her." I never knew what she meant. When she got pregnant, everything was beautiful. I would rub her stomach to feel my baby girl. I talked to her the whole time she was inside her mother. She would kick my hand at the sound of my voice. I fell in love with her before she even got here.

I was headed to one more meeting out of town to finalize my promotion to be the CEO of our company out in New York, at the corporate office, when Lisa went into labor. She had asked me not to go the night before, but it was a big move for us. Higher pay, plus the baby wasn't due for another week and a half. So, I had more time—well, I thought I did.

The baby came in the middle of a two-hour delay to my flight back home. When I received the call, I was excited, and I knew I had time. My mother and father were with Lisa, so she wasn't alone. Cory was with the family as well. No one called to tell me my little girl didn't make it.

I reached the recovery room with flowers and balloons and the biggest smile a proud new father could wear. I was yelled at, cursed out, accused of cheating—all in one breath and in front of all my family. I could have walked out on her. She didn't console me, hold me, or even ask me if I was all right. Not only that. She didn't want me around her for a long time. So, I would wait until late at night and go cry and talk to God in the nursery.

She seemed so unhappy with everything I did. She would fuss about the smallest things and made me feel like less of a man, not knowing how I felt and what it was doing to me. She treated me as if I hadn't lost my baby. She acted as if I didn't have feelings and was being selfish and only cared about hers. What took the cake away from me is when she asked me for a divorce.

As I boarded the flight and relaxed myself, the flight attendant stated she would accommodate my needs and told me to enjoy the flight.

All I could think about was Michelle. I couldn't wait to get to her. Like a kid, I was watching the clock and rushing the flight. I wanted nothing more than to have her in my arms. That soft voice in my ear. I was falling hard for her and praying for a safe flight to her and from her. I also prayed she would say, "Forget my life" and move in with me. I didn't want to rush her, but I didn't want to take it slow either.

She was the best feeling I had ever felt, and I wanted it forever.

Once we landed, I called Cory and told him I had made it. Then I called my mother so she wouldn't worry. I called Michelle, but she didn't answer. I called again, and still no answer, so I walked down to baggage claim and gathered my things. I called her once more, but my baby didn't answer. I started to get worried about her not answering, so I got Cory to call his girl to see what the problem was. It took him a long minute to get back at me. Here was, at this airport waiting, and it was starting to feel like she was standing me up. I called her phone once more. Still no answer.

I called Cory back to see what was wrong and why they weren't answering. He said Kerry wouldn't pick up for him. I started to think, was they playing us, or did something happen to them? I got kind of upset with myself for thinking this was real, but I didn't want to give up on her, so I waited until my cousin called me to see what Kerry said. What I got next was not the phone call I was expecting. Kerry had to drive over to Michelle's house to see why she wasn't answering. I started to worry about her. Was she sleeping and didn't hear the phone, or did something happen to her? Does she have a man, and was she selling me a dream? What in the hell was going on? I was about to book another flight back home when Cory called and said the police were at Michelle's house. Something had happened to her. I canceled my ticket back and told him to tell Kerry could she come get me or give me the address to the hospital. I thought that would take too long, so I took a cab to the hospital where my heart was.

My adrenaline was rushing, and my heart was beating out of my chest. *What happened?* I thought. *Did she get sick? Did she fall?* A million and one questions rushed through my head. I just had to wait until I got to her. Once I arrived at the hospital, I paid the cab, then rushed in. I had my luggage still at the airport. I told them I'd call them with the address so they could send it on request.

I walked to information to give them Michelle's name. I knew it was going to be awhile due to all the people in the waiting area. Once they looked her up, they told me there was nothing they could tell me because I wasn't a relative. Walking to the waiting area, I sat there for a while before I saw Kerry rushing into the hospital doors. She had worry in her eyes.

"I saw her go inside the house. Then I drove off," she said. She started to cry, and I told her to calm down. She sat next to me, then jumped up stood in line, and waited to talk to the receptionist.

Waiting behind an upset woman, I could tell she was getting frustrated. Approaching the desk, she asked for an update on Michelle. The lady made a phone call, then said they were moving her to ICU recovery and that we could wait upstairs. She also said a detective was on the way to ask questions. Kerry had worry in her eyes. I asked her whether Michelle had a boyfriend on our way toward the elevator doors. She said no, not since 2015. The same thing Michelle had told me. So why would a detective be looking to ask us questions? I wondered, but I paid it no mind. I waited patiently for the elevator doors to open.

Once we walked inside the elevator, a guy walked up aggressively and stopped the doors from closing. He started talking to Kerry and asked who I was. I didn't know who the hell he was, but I was listening to every word he had to say. If he was the one who did this to my baby, we were going to have a very bad misunderstanding.

An hour went by, and once the doctor approached us with the detective, he told us she had been severely beaten. Did we know of anyone who she might have had an altercation with? Kerry told them no, and he looked at me and asked where I had been earlier tonight. I told him I had been on a flight here. I then continued to tell him I just had bought a cab for this ride. I asked him why I was being questioned. He answered, "The way she was beaten, only a man can do that." My heart broke, and my knees went weak. I had to sit down. I was confused as to why. Who could have done her this way? She was soft and sweet, a real nice woman. I was in rage and in pain for her.

If I find out who was behind this, I am going to do all I can to make sure they never hurt anyone again.

I asked the doctor if I could see her. He told me the odds of her not waking up. I asked if I could stay with her so she wouldn't be alone. He answered yes, and said we could both visit her, but only one of us could stay overnight. Kerry was crying so hard, I hugged her to console her feelings. But the guy moved me out of the way quick enough to hold her. I'm thinking he was the guy who cheated on her, because she didn't want him on her. I paid it no attention. Hell, I had other shit to deal with. I was upset and wanted the person who had done this to her to pay.

I called Cory once the detective had gone, and while we were on our way to her room. The fella who Kerry was with stayed in the waiting room area. Cory asked whether he needed to come down here, and I told him he needed to check with Kerry. I didn't let him know she was with some guy. I just told him I was straight but if he wanted to ask her, he could.

When we got to her door, my heart was racing. I wasn't mentally ready for what I was about to see. I walked closer to her bed. I held back my tears and told Kerry I had to step out for a second. I barely made it to the hallway before I started crying. My sweet baby was all beaten up, swollen. She was covered from head to toe in bandages. My heart broke, and I cried. Yes, you heard me: I cried. Whoever did this to her was a monster. I had to pull myself together. I called Cory back and told him how bad she was.

He heard it in my voice that I had been crying. He told me to hang on; he was on his way. I gave him the address to this hospital. Then I called my mother to tell her the bad news. Once she answered the phone, I broke down.

"Momma, someone here in Arkansas beat up Michelle really bad."

"Tony, calm down, baby. Tell me what happened," she said, as I could barely talk. I told her everything that had happened from the time I had gotten off the phone with her to the time I showed up to the hospital.

"Oh no, baby. I'm sorry to hear that. Are her parents there with her?" she asked.

I walked to the room to ask Kerry if her parents knew about this. She said her parents had died returning from Paris in a private jet. My heart hurt even worse for her. Here she was, alone in this world, with no parents. I held back my tears when she mentioned it to me. I never thought to ask her about her parents. Walking back into the hallway, I told my mother what Kerry had told me.

"Aw, poor thing," my mother said, her tone dropping. "We will be on the first flight to you, baby. We will be her family now. Your father is sleeping, and I don't want to wake him, but I will call and order our tickets first thing tomorrow," she said. She told me she loved me, and we hung up. I rushed back to Michelle's side, holding her finger because that was the only thing I could grab.

I felt so bad for this woman, and I also felt angry. I asked her to stay one more week. If she had of stayed, this wouldn't have been going on. I put the channel on sports and turned it down low. Kerry asked where the rest of my luggage was. I told her I had left it at the airport. She asked if I needed to get it. I told her that I would have it sent to Michelle's later. If I paid it, they would hold it. I had my business case with me as well as my laptop. I could still work from where I was. She asked if I was hungry, and I said no, I was fine. I had so many emotions rushing through my head, I knew I wasn't going to get any sleep. I just kept my eye on my baby while she laid here in a coma. I wished there was something I could do. I felt so helpless. I was relieved that my family was standing with me and supporting Michelle and me.

Once Kerry left to go home, I got on my knees and prayed. I talked to God about this woman until the sun came up. I called my boss and told him I had an emergency. He gave me a week off to be with my family. He said if I needed anything, I could call him. If I had to spend money, he said use the company card.

It was about mid-morning. I went to the cafeteria to buy myself a breakfast sandwich and a large coffee. I hurried back to Michelle just as Kerry was walking in. Cory arrived at the same as my parents. When my mother entered the room, she touched Michelle's head and prayed for her. She then told all of us to grab hands and pray as well. When we finished, she walked over to me and hugged me and said the Lord told her Michelle would pull through. That made me feel better, because once my mother said God told her, I knew it was true. Kerry was happy to see Cory and my mother. She took my parents out for lunch and drove them to a hotel to freshen up. I ordered a rental off the company card just in case they wanted to sightsee while they were here.

I couldn't believe this was happening. I kept asking who could have done this to her. What man did she have in her life who hated her so much he'd try to kill her?

Later that evening, the same detective came and talked to us about some information they had. Kerry was pulled to the side and asked questions on Michelle's whereabouts before she came home. They traced her credit card and found charges made from a car-rental company back in Texas. They were getting a court order for the videotapes to be released. That might provide a lead as to who picked up the car.

My mother overheard them talking about a cosmetic line that she wears. She came back and asked me whether I knew that Michelle was the owner of Dreams and the daughter of the founder of the name-brand cosmetic line. I had no idea. I told my mother Michelle didn't brag about having money. She wasn't even a big spender unless it was for a good cause. She did mention that she was maintaining her parents' house as well as her own. We walked arm in arm around the hospital, talking about Michelle. My mother knew I really cared about her. Then I walked and talked with my dad. He questioned my feelings for Michelle just to see how I would react. My father had his way of finding things out. When he saw how humble I was about him grilling me, he said that it had something to do with Michelle.

Only a soft and selfless woman can bring out the calmness in a man. That's why he chose my mother. He knew she was sweet, kindhearted, and giving just by how I reacted to him judging my care for her. Once we made it back to the room, he told me he supported my decision no matter what. He also told me a jealous man will do this to a woman if he doesn't want her to leave him. So, I asked Kerry what DeWayne's last name was, but before I could finish, she said he was still in prison. I've already mentioned him. I sat next to Michelle and asked her to wake up for me.

She didn't respond, so I kissed her and fell asleep right next to her. With my family here by my side, I got the rest I needed to be strong for my woman. I said I wasn't going to leave her side until they found the person responsible. I was going to have them pay for what they did to her.

CHAPTER 22

Michelle. Dreaming inside a coma. After she was beaten, she cried for help. The pain was unbearable, so she fell into a deep slumber.

I was having the time of my life. Tony and I were swimming in the hotel pool. We raced, and I kept winning. He was so much fun to be around. After that, we showered and fed each other takeout. He was just what I needed at this point in my life. I needed me a man, because all work and no play had gotten lonely when I went to bed at night. I wanted to share my world with someone, but not just anybody. No, he had to be on my level and on the same page. I wanted a family so I could pass my inheritance down to my child, the same as my mother and father had done for me.

"I want to ask you something, Michelle, and I want you to be honest with me," Tony said. "Do you feel I make you happy?"

"Yes, you do, my love," I replied.

"You make me very happy. In fact, I'm so happy I haven't gone home yet," I said with a big smile.

"Happy enough to marry me?" he asked as he got down on one knee.

"You want to marry me, Tony?" I asked as joy filled my heart, and I began to cry.

"Yes, Michelle. I want us to be as one. I've never met anyone who makes me happy to be alive. Your spirit is refreshing as well as magnetic. Your energy sucks me into your zone, and all I want to do is be wherever you are, making you smile and giving you the family, you always hint at wanting. I could do those things for you. All I need you to do for me is trust that I will never do anything to hurt you. You give me a feeling deep down inside that makes me want to be a man you can count on, someone you can depend on."

As he was telling me all those sweet somethings, I felt so loved at that moment.

"Yes, yes, I will marry you," I answered.

That day, we went out for a walk. The sky was deep blue and the clouds puffy white. The grass was a vibrant green, and the flowers were so colorful. The wind felt like a soft breeze across my face. We walked the park listening to the birds sing, sounds like they are enjoying the weather as much as we are. It was an amazing feeling to be loved so purely by this man. Something I had never felt before.

We played alone in the park like little kids, running, jumping, chasing each other around. I was smiling; he was smiling. Nothing could come in between us at this point. We were head over hills for each other. We walked back to the hotel hand in hand and sat around in the lobby. We laughed and talked about some of the people in the lobby. I rushed to his suite to be alone with him and to give him a part of me only he could have.

That night, I slept in his arms. I felt safe, warm, loved, and secure, knowing no one was going to hurt me. When I opened my eyes, I couldn't see where I was or who I was with, but I felt someone lift me off the floor and onto a bed. My head was pounding, and my body ached badly. I tried to speak, but I couldn't. I tried opening my eyes, but it was too painful. I began to cry from agony all over me. What happened to me? Where were these people taking me? I had no idea what to make of this sudden pain. I thought about Tony. Was he in this pain with me? I called for help, but no one answered. I cried and cried, but it felt like no one was listening. I need answers, and I needed them fast. Then I fell back to sleep not knowing what had happened. I passed out and began to sleep once more.

I opened my eyes to the voice of Tony asking me to squeeze his finger if I could hear him. I tried to open my eyes, but the dim lights hurt my head and eyes. I was in so much pain all over my body. I heard voices that I didn't know. I wanted to say something to Tony, but I fell asleep.

"Hey, baby."

"Hi, Momma. Where is Daddy?" I asked.

"Sh, baby, it's not time for you to see Daddy yet," my mother said in a soft voice.

"But I miss him. I miss you," I said as I began to cry. "Why is he hiding from me. I need him to see me. I need to talk to him. I met a guy, and he makes me happy. I just wanted to introduce him to my friend," I said as I began to cry some more.

"Baby, it's not time for you to see him. I'm here to make sure you get back in time."

"In time for what, Momma? Where are we? Where do I need to go? I want to stay with you. I don't want to go back. It hurts," I said as I started to shake my head no. She began to fade right in front of my eyes.

Opening my eyes again, I could hear a woman praying for me to be okay. It sounded like she was talking to the Lord about me. I fell asleep again. This time I didn't see my mother or my father. I felt lonely and confused as to what was going on with me. It felt like a dream that I couldn't wake up from. I couldn't calculate what was going on, but I remember hearing voices. I even thought I heard people crying and talking to me. I was trying to wake up, but every time I awoke, I fell right back to sleep.

I felt a hand inside mine. I opened my eyes for a split second and saw Tony. I tried to smile, but the pain in my face was excruciating, so I went numb and fell back to sleep.

"Baby, you are going to have to fight a little harder," my mother said.

"Momma, you're back!" I said excitedly. She had a disappointed look on her face. I asked why she was upset with me. She said she wasn't; she was just tired and needed to get back to Daddy. I asked if I could go with her to see him. Once again, she said it wasn't time. It grew dark, and I couldn't see anything.

I heard a woman once again, talking to the Lord, asking him to protect me from all harm and to allow his unfailing love to be with her son. I was confused as to why she was talking to him about me, and who was her son? I tried to open my eyes, but it hurt too badly, so I dozed off. This time no dreams, no parents. It felt cold; then it got hot. Then the pain came again, then it left. Sleep was all I could do, so I slept, and I slept. I wish I knew what was happening to me, why it was so fuzzy.

I started thinking I was dead, and God had closed me out of heaven. It felt like I had slept for eternity. Then I felt a hand slide back into mine. I opened my eyes again to see Tony once more. I tried to say hi, but the pain was unbearable, so I just closed my eyes and went back to sleep. I then dreamed of walking inside my house and being attacked by someone there. I tried to fight back, but I was thrown around like a ragdoll from wall to wall, hitting the floor, and I felt fists pounding me all over. Then I woke up, blaring and crying. I asked for help over and over, but no one came to me. I cried and I cried, until I passed out.

I dreamed this dream over and over, until I started praying to God. I prayed for him to help me. I didn't know what was going on and why I was going through this. I felt something warm on my lips, so I opened my eyes. This time, I saw Tony. He was kissing me. He then put Chapstick on my lips. I stared into his eyes as he smiled at me. He then began to cry. I didn't know why he looked so sad. I wondered why I couldn't move. That's when I saw KK smiling at me with tears in her eyes. I tried to talk, but my mouth wouldn't move, and the pain was still intolerable.

A doctor came to wave a bright light in my eyes. Which, by the way, was unbearable! He touched other places on me that were also agonizing to the touch. He then placed a hand on my thumb and pushed, but it felt numb.

I saw Tony's face once more. I tried to smile, but it hurt even to move my face. Then I went to sleep. I dreamed of talking to my mother again. She told me this was the last time I would see her. She also said that she was proud of me and she knew I could do it. I didn't understand what she was talking about. All I knew was she was disappearing, but before she left, she told me that my dad said that he was proud of me. He also said that the young man by my side was someone I could count on. I began to cry, telling both my parents I loved them. Then I went to sleep, and this time, I slept for a long time.

Pushing that button that was stuck to my thumb kept my body from hurting.

When I opened my eyes, I saw a woman I didn't know. She smiled a soft, pretty smile. She then rubbed things on my face, saying, "There, there, child. You are safe now. You are in our hands. We will protect you." Through the pain, I tried to smile and tried to ask her who she was, but she just kept on washing my face.

I noticed KK's mother had come to look at me. She smiled and then started crying, and she kept saying, "You poor thing. Who did this to you?"

Once I woke up again, I was looking for Tony. There was no one here and moving my head from side to side to find him was getting painful. *Where did everyone go?* I thought to myself, so I closed my eyes. As I slept and slept. I remembered walking into my house and being attacked. My face was covered, and I swung, hitting the intruder. Then I know I heard him say, "Aw, hell naw, bitch!" Then he started throwing me from wall to wall. One hard blow to my face, and I could feel my jaw breaking. Picking me up and slamming me to the floor and pounding on me some more.

I woke up to a woman standing over me with coco-complexed skin and a mean look on her face. She was mouthing off, but her words weren't clear. She then went to place a pillow on my face as if she was going to smother me. Helpless in this situation, I could do nothing but lay there.

I was right. She started smothering me. Not knowing who this woman was or why she was doing this to me, I made sure I got a great look at her face. Who knows? This might have been one of the intruders coming back to finish me off. But what did I do to deserve what they were doing to me? Who was she, and why was she here?

A knock on the door, then a click, someone calling out my name. Suddenly, I felt pressure being released from my face as I gasped for air. When I opened my eyes, I could see images of a group of people walking into the doorway.

She was acting like she was making me comfortable. They all showered me with flowers and balloons, get-well cards, and teddy bears.

I dreamed of being attacked every time I fell asleep. I slept some more, but every time I felt Tony's hand in mine, I opened my eyes. Every time I looked around, I saw someone different, but this time, I saw a man looked just looked at me. I didn't know who he was, but he kept an eye on me as he felt my face. He was mumbling something that sounded like a prayer. He then asked if I was okay and said to squeeze his hand if I knew who he was.

I didn't squeeze. He then asked me to squeeze his hand if I knew Tony. The last question was "Do you have feelings for my son, Tony?" I gave a light squeeze. He went on praying, then he asked, "Do you believe in God?" He placed his hands in mine, and I squeezed his hand tighter than before. He smiled and said, "Welcome to the family, baby. We will take care of you now."

Then a woman came and smiled and said, "We will look out for you now. Please get some rest and get well so you can come back to us.

CHAPTER 23

Something Is a Little Off

Amanda

I woke up this morning feeling a little different. I had been talking to Jeff for about a week now. He had me so happy and excited about being his new friend. We have so many things in common, like we both love action movies, swimming, and going to the gym. He writes poems in his spare time and when he is inspired. I had something to do with him being inspired now.

As I walked into my kitchen to start a pot of coffee, I noticed the news was saying a well-known owner from the cosmetic line Dream had been severely beaten and was fighting for her life. My heart stopped when I heard that her home had been invaded and she had been attacked. I rushed to shower and got dress. I called Jeff to tell him the bad news and to ask him what I should do to help my friend.

My phone buzzed with a call. I answered it. It was my mother, asking me if I'd seen the news. We talked, and I told her I was on my way home. I told her I would be there later in the evening.

Forgetting I had Jeff on the line, I asked him to call me back, or I'd call him once I had gotten on the road. I was puzzled. Who could have done this to her? I know I was upset that she was so close to Kerry, but hey, she still was there for me. She was still someone I would help in a bad situation. I had a hard time fighting through traffic. Once I had gone outside the city limits, which was to hours of heavy morning traffic, I rushed through those small towns in a hurry to get to my friend. I was speeding and very glad that there wasn't a cop in sight.

I stopped to get gas and rest for lunch. Then I was back in traffic. I made it to Little Rock at 4 p.m. due to the traffic that took place this morning and around lunch. I was happy I made it. Calling around from hospital to hospital, I found out where she was. I then called my mother to see if she was coming. She announced she was away on business. I was rushing her while we were on the phone earlier. I didn't pay attention to her when she asked if I could go in place of her. She had flowers and a card sent to Michelle's room, so that is how I found her.

I waited on the elevator to stop on her floor. I was hoping I didn't run into Kerry. I didn't want to deal with my feelings for her during my visit with Michelle. As the doors to the waiting area opened outside Michelle's room, to my surprise, not only did I find Kerry, but I found Tony, his mother, and his father in the waiting room. I wasn't ready for this. I didn't even want them to see me. But here I was, walking right into the midst of them.

"Amanda, why are you here?" Kerry yelled as she walked up to me with anger in her face.

"I saw on the news that Michelle was hurt, so I rushed here as soon as I could to show her some support," I replied in the calmest voice I could muster.

I did not want to put on a show because my heart was sad for Michelle, so I kept walking to see her. When I approached her room, my heart dropped. I walked closer to her bed. My lifelong friend was lying in that bed, fighting for her life. She was all bandaged up, as if someone had broken every bone in her body. As I looked at her, I began to cry, while thinking to myself, *What kind of monster would do this?* She was one of the nicest people I knew. I just looked at her from head to toe, wishing she would open her eyes.

I sat down in the seat next to her and began to cry.

"You can't leave me here all by myself. You are my friend, more like a sister. You always check up on me when I moved away for college. When I was down and out, needing money for food or my books. You helped me get through school with no hesitation, always smiling and joking about crazy things that I would tell you happened to me. You kept me looking at the bright side of things. I feel bad about what I did to Kerry and Drake. I miss Kerry, and we would still be friends if I had not taken it all out on her. I miss all of us, including Allen."

I was talking to her and crying out for her to understand that I needed her to make it out of this alive. Other than my mother and brothers, she was the only true friend I had. I had Lisa, but lately, she had been treating me like I didn't exist.

"I know I am far from perfect, Michelle, but I promise I will make it up to Kerry. I promise I will be true and sincere when I apologize to her. I really do miss how we all used to hang. I want that back. I talked to my mother. She said she would come and visit you when she returns to the state. She told me to say a prayer for you," I told her as I got down on my knees.

Kerry walked in. I looked at her with tears in my eyes and asked her to forgive me.

"Kerry, I know what I had done was wrong, and I understand if you don't forgive me. But I do want you to know that I am so sorry. I was about to pray for Michelle. I would like it if you prayed with me, please."

She looked at me with shock in her eyes, and she didn't say a word. She just got down on her knees, and we began to pray. We prayed for a long time, and when we stood on our feet, she looked at me and said, "Are you for real, Amanda? Or do you feel sorry for Michelle and want to be nice?" Her tone was full of mistrust.

"I'm for real, Kerry. I miss you guys. I was just jealous of you and Michelle's friendship. I felt like an outsider when it came to her. She made me feel more like her friend than you made me feel like yours. I know I didn't make it easy when Allen died, and I ran off to college with hate for you in my heart. But I still remember the fun times we had, all the wild and crazy things we used to do. I do really miss you," I told her with a sincere heart.

"What made you want to apologize to me suddenly? Like it took Michelle to get beat for you to come to me and apologize? Why should I forgive you after I caught you with Drake? Better yet, how do I know you wasn't the one who did this to Michelle? Who do you think I wanted to be around the most when we both lost Allen? Did you for once stop and think, maybe she needs me? Or maybe, since I am his twin sister, I need to comfort her because she did love him? Did it ever occur to you that the first boy I fell in love with and gave my virginity to suddenly died on me?" Kerry said, frustrated and all out of breath.

"You have no idea how hard it was for me to go on day by day missing him, and you treating me like it was all my fault. I understand I was at fault for falling asleep—I do—and I hate that I fell asleep. I dreamed about it repeatedly for years at night, wishing I could go back and stay awake. I missed him, and I wanted only him. I missed you. We were all a team, not just me and Michelle but *all of us*!"

As she finished, we both just looked at each other. Then she walked out of the room without saying another word.

I didn't blame her if she wants nothing to do with me. I gave her many reasons not to, so if she didn't want to forgive me, she didn't have to. That was not going to stop me from playing nice. This was only the beginning, and I wasn't going to give up. I would just give her some time.

I looked at Michelle and kissed her hand and told her my mother and I would be back to see her. I told her I love her, and I asked her to stay with us.

Leaving the hospital, I saw Drake approaching the cafeteria area. I slipped right passed him, not wanting him to see me. I had to let him go if I wanted Kerry to understand how for real, I was about my apology and how much I wanted us all to be friends. I know it was too soon for me to ask her, but I had to. It felt like the perfect opportunity to do so.

~

Later, after I had a shower and was back in my old room, I walked past my twin's door. It had been years since I had been in his room. My heart was hammering when I grabbed the doorknob. I opened the door, and his room was the same way he had left it. A tear filled my eye, and I began to cry and talk to my brother. I cried harder when I saw all the photos he had of Michelle, Kerry, and me, thick as thieves. I missed those days like crazy, and I needed to heal as well. I found some of the letters Kerry had written to him in a box of pictures he had of her by herself. I thought about giving them to her as a peace offering. I needed her to know I meant what I said.

My cell phone rang, scaring the shit out of me. I ran back to my room just in time to answer for Jeff.

"Hello."

"Hello, my sweet cake, how are you holding up?" he asked.

"I'm better now that I am home. I saw my friend. She was beaten very badly. I didn't know she had enemies that would want to see her dead. She was always kind and giving to others, even if they weren't worth her being nice to," I said in a sad tone.

"Well, is the cops looking for the person who done it?" he asked.

"Yes, I do believe so. Hell, I hope so. I hope they find them and charge them with attempted murder for how badly she was beaten."

"Me too, baby. Me too," he said as his voice went soft. "How long are you going to be home?" he asked.

"I really can't say. I want to be here when she awakes so she can see that I am here to support her."

"You are such a good friend. I wonder how good of a girlfriend you'd be?" he said as his voice took on a flirty sound.

"Boy, you so crazy," I said, as he had put a smile on my face. "I wish you here. I could use some good company," I said as I rubbed on my teddy bear that my dad had gotten me when I lost my first tooth.

"So, do I, but unfortunately, I have a very busy day tomorrow, and the day after," he said as he cleared his throat. "I am free this weekend if you want to make dinner reservations for us back at the hotel. You know, the place where we met."

"Yes, sure thing. I have a taste for those roasted carrots with the wild rice and salmon. That was very good," I said, nodding my head as if he could see. We talked a little while longer. Then I fell asleep watching a movie. He had given me something good to look forward to this weekend. I was really feeling this guy, and I needed no one to get in the way of my happiness. I know I had done a lot of wrong things, but I was trying to right them so I could move on in a better state of mind. I was looking forward to becoming a better person.

The next morning, I found my mother at the dinner table with a recorder in her hands. I must have frightened her when I said, "What's that?" pulling the chair away from the table and taking a seat.

"Oh, Amanda, honey, you scared me!"

"Sorry, Momma. Good morning. What is that, work?" I finished my question from before.

"No, baby. It's a message I saved from your brother."

"My twin?" I said, up outta my seat.

"Yes, dear. He called me that night when you guys were on your way back home. I missed it because I had taken a shower and fallen asleep."

"Really? What's it says? Play it, Momma," I begged her.

"Okay, shh, listen," she said.

"Hey, Momma, we are on our way home. We had such a great time. We met some new friends and went on a yacht. Amanda is in the back sleeping, I am driving, Michelle is sleeping in back, and Kerry is awake upfront with me. I miss you guys, and I love you too. We will be home soon. Kisses." As the recorder kept playing, I could hear him tell Kerry he was in love with her and she had shown him the best time of his life. He then went on to tell her if she was sleepy, she could go to sleep.

She said, "No, I am going to stay up with you. Then, when I can't fight my sleep any longer, I will wake up Amanda since she was the first to sleep. We all made a promise, and I will keep that."

"I love you. Do you know that, girl?" he said to Kerry.

"Yes, I do been knowing it for a long time now. I love you too."

It sounded like they shared a kiss, and then the message ended. My heart dropped to the floor, and I began to cry uncontrollably. My brother was very much in love, and it wasn't her fault. All this time I was running around blaming her, and she was innocent. I sat there in my mother's arms and cried like a baby, both from hearing his voice and from knowing I did her wrong.

I had no idea this had taken place. Had I showed a little more compassion, maybe we all could have still been friends. I went back to my old room and laid across my bed feeling down and out, with my mind full of thoughts and what-ifs. I never knew he had told her to go to sleep. I also didn't know that he loved her and that she loved him just as much. I felt horrible. I needed for Kerry to know, and I needed her forgiveness. But I know she hates me, because all this time, I was trying to hurt her.

CHAPTER 24

Detective Randy Hall and Detective Vincent Banks—Insight on the Case

Randy Hall

I was called on the dispatch about a breaking and entering at the victim's home. I arrived at the scene ten minutes later. As I approached the front door, I didn't see any signs of forced entry, so I knocked hard on the already opened door and proceeded to enter, giving my name and authority to approach the living room/foyer as I proceeded to the nearest hallway.

That is where I saw Michelle lying on the ground in a small puddle of blood that was coming from her face. She was still breathing but unconscious, so I didn't move her. I called for backup from my dispatch. That is when the neighbor walked in, yelling, "I had to go home and call 911. I found her just lying here. I was worried because the door was wide open." As she told me what she knew, I made a report.

The ambulance showed up nine minutes after I sent out the request. They approached the victim and loaded her onto the stretcher. I finished making my way through the house and still saw no signs of entry. I walked down to the basement, and that is when I found broken glass on the floor, in front of the back door.

I made the report of a breaking and entering, as well as a battery case to be opened and investigated. Someone wanted this woman dead, and I had to find out who it was and why they had committed this crime. As I looked at the photos hanging around in her home, I noticed she was very beautiful, and she was the daughter of the famous Eleanor Dream from Dreams cosmetics.

This is a famous brand that my wife uses. I searched around for more evidence to find out who could have done this to this lady. As I made my way back to the front door, I saw a young woman reporting that she had dropped the victim off after a road trip. She was in tears and appeared to be shaken by the scene. I made my way to her to ask some questions so I could try to puzzle in some of the missing pieces.

Later that evening, a call came through the station reporting a vehicle abandoned in a ditch, four blocks from the victim's house. I knew then I had a lead in the case. I ran the tags and found that it was from a rental company in Texas. I called the company and asked if they were missing a 2017 Acura ILX (white).

I proceeded to ask them to check their files to see who had rented the vehicle. They put me through hell for the information I needed, until I told them a crime had been committed and the person who rented the car might have played a part in it.

I was surprised to discover that the vehicle had been rented in the victim's name. What I didn't understand was why, so I took a trip to the hospital to see if anyone had any information.

When I arrived, I saw a well-known detective talking to the doctor assigned to the victim. I gave him the information I had to see if he would let me in on the case. He told me he was a close friend of the victim's father. I asked about her parents to see if I needed to get ahold of them. He went on to say that they had died in a plane crash coming home from Paris, France. Very sad news to hear. I asked if there was anything, I could do to help us find the person responsible for hurting this young woman. He then told me to investigate the rental place to see if they had video of the person who picked the car up from the enterprise. I got right on it and made my way to the station, asking for permission to send for a search warrant and to confiscate the video of the person who picked up the keys to the vehicle. This was going to take some time, so I went ahead and filed a report on the information I had. I kept thinking about this young lady whom I had found. Somehow, she was stuck in my mind, and I felt so sorry for her.

I was happy she was still alive when I found her. I waited until my cell phone rang with the judge giving me permission to take the warrant to the detective at the hospital with the victim. He was the first one to arrive at the victim's house. As I approached him, I greeted him, and then I said, "I talked to your boss and told him you would be securing the premises and to keep a close eye on the victim while Detective Jeff, who, by the way, is head of national security, and I make our way to Texas to obtain the evidence I need to put whoever is responsible behind bars." We agreed, and then I headed out to see my wife and pack a small suitcase to head out to Texas. I knew I was going to be there overnight since the rental place would be closed. I called my partner to let him know I was outside. We headed out of the state to gather what I hoped would be good evidence.

Vincent Banks

As I walked into the waiting room area to wait to see my deceased best friend's daughter, a very sad emotion came over me. This was a nice family with values and good upbringing. They were trustworthy friends. I couldn't imagine her having enemies who would want her dead. I told the nurses' station to put her under private care. I didn't want to risk the suspect coming back for her. I told them if they didn't know her parents' name or a trusted friend, then they were not to see her. I went on my laptop and looked over the reports that the other officers had made. Still in the waiting room area waiting to see how badly beaten she was, I was going to get to the bottom of this if it was the last thing I did. I had to keep my personal feelings under wraps, because they would take me off the case if I lost my head.

I had to find out who wanted Michelle dead. What kind of trouble was this young lady in? As I did my paperwork electronically, I was offered a nice hot cup of coffee by one of the nurses. It was just what I had needed, because I knew I wasn't going to sleep until I found out who the criminal was in this case. I wasn't prepared to hear what the doctor was saying about her conditions. Hall found her just in the nick of time. She had suffered from broken bones, a cracked rib, and a sprained ankle. Her face was swollen and puffy, and she was in a mild coma from head injuries. They had to run more CT scans to make sure nothing was permanently damaged. I asked the doctor how long she was going to be in a coma. He said it could be days, weeks, maybe even months. However, it shouldn't be much longer than that. He then told me that she would be in and out until she fully recovered because she was heavily sedated so she would feel less pain in her head. They had to monitor her head often due to the swelling. However, she would recover in time.

I asked how long I had before I could visit, but he told me to give her a few hours to rest. When he came back from checking on her, she could have visitors. I was relieved when he told me she was going to recover. I just didn't want to see anything happen to her. I called my wife to let her know I would be waiting and working from the hospital. She understood the many reasons I had and came to show support. We have known Michelle all her life. We went to college together, and my wife is the reason her parents got together. She set them up on a blind date with us. We all became very good friends. Kelly and I couldn't have children, so we would spend time with Michelle all the time. I must admit, with both of us so dedicated to our careers, we lost time, so we spent less time with her after her parents passed. However, we made it our own business to be there for her when she needed us.

My cell phone vibrated. It was Hall. He said he was two hours outside the town where the suspect had picked up the vehicle.

"The place will be closed by the time I get there, but I will be there first thing in the morning," Detective Hall stated.

"Good, I'm still here with the victim now. I read the report from the other officers, and now I'm looking into the credit card company to see if they have a record of any other transaction." I told him to check back once he retrieved the video.

Later, I saw Michelle's best friend Kerry along with a couple of guys. I knew that only a man could have hurt her as badly as she was. The doctor was approaching the guest who had been waiting on Michelle to come out of recovery. I waited until the doctor made his announcement, and then I confronted one of the guys and asked questions. What made me seek out him as a suspect was the tone of his physique. He was a, well, fit kind of guy. She was a small woman, and he seemed to fit as a suspect, as someone who could have hurt a person of her size. After his story checked out, I crossed him off my list. I made my way to Michelle's room. I was saddened when I saw her helpless body lying in that bed.

I had to keep my composure and not let my personal feelings get the best of me. Here was this young lady fighting for her life, looking so helpless. I allowed the others to visit as I made my way back to my temporary workstation. I checked in with Hall to see if he had made it.

That morning after I left Michelle's room, I called Detective Hall to get the scoop. He was retaining the evidence and was heading back to the state as we spoke. I needed answers about the perpetrator who did this to my best friend's baby girl. I headed to the station for a little to talk with the chief.

As time moved forward, Hall was back in town, and we viewed the tape. Once we clocked the time of the call and the transaction, we noticed a woman picking up the car. The only thing we didn't see was her face. As we manipulated the video, looking at all angles, we could not get a good look at who she was.

We could only tell she was a woman by her body. She had a scarf tied around her face and sunglasses over her eyes. We gave what we had to the reporter from Channel 7 and told her to ask if anyone knows this woman. As of right now, all we can do is wait, hoping someone knows who she is calls the police if they see her. We put up a reward for any good information to crack this case.

CHAPTER 25

What Are You Going to Do about Him?

Kerry

Never in a million years did I think Amanda would come to her senses. We already dealt with one death. I guess Michelle's attack hit too close to home. Now she has had a change of heart after she tried to ruin my life. What she doesn't know is she did me a favor. She helped me get over Drake's lying, cheating ass.

Even though I was mad at Amanda for taking my man, Drake was dead wrong. He was my man. We lived together, and I'd put up with a lot. But since he can't keep his dick in his pants, I don't need to be with him. I don't want to catch any type of STD or AIDS. And he's so stupid, he didn't even know she was just using him to get back at me.

Now he's crying like a bitch since I won't take him back. I can't. I won't allow myself to do it. I know my worth now, and I know Drake doesn't deserve me. He says he love me, but he doesn't. When you love someone, you want to see them happy. You want to be the one to make them happy.

Never again. I'm done with that. I had to pick up the rest of my things from the house and let him know what's up so I could move on with my life. Now, Cory is no angel, but at least he was honest about what he had done wrong in his past relationship.

Meanwhile, Michelle is still in a coma, and she had a good man by her side who wasn't leaving until she woke up. For having been single so long, it didn't take her long to find a good man. She had been through a lot in her life at a young age. God knew what he was doing. Since she was still sleeping, I figured I would run home, hoping that by the time I made it back, she'd be waking up.

I slowly grabbed my suitcase and filled it neatly with my things. All I wanted was my stuff, that I could carry off to where I was going. He could have everything else. I really did not want the memories of Drake and me in my new space. I didn't really feel up to arguing, so I placed my headphones in my ear. But that made matters worse once he came in and saw me packing.

"Kerry, what are you doing?"

"What does it look like I'm doing, Drake?"

"You going somewhere? When are you coming back?"

"Never!"

"Whoa, wait a minute! You call yourself leaving me?"

"Yes, that's what I am doing."

"You not going anywhere, so you can put that shit back up! But we didn't discuss this. We never had a chance to talk! Now you're just going to come in here, pack your things, and leave."

"Yes, just like that, the same way we didn't discuss you fucking Amanda behind my back!"

"Why do you have to be so damn smart! You know I love you and I will do anything for you. Why do you want to give up on us?"

"You gave up on us the moment you allowed another woman into your life! So, please do not come at me with that I'm-giving-up-on-us shit, Drake. This is all you!"

We were both yelling back and forth at one another, as if we didn't have neighbors. I know they must have heard us, because we were getting louder and louder. I know that this was hurting him, but it was the only way I could be happy. I can't overlook my own happiness while keeping him happy. It's not working that way.

I must do what's right for me, and that is to move on.

"So, you're just going to leave me here alone?"

"Yes, Drake. That way, you can be free to do anything you want."

"I don't want to do anything but be with you."

"Look, Drake, this is not easy for me, but you seem to like other women while you're with me. Watch how much easier it is going to be when you don't have to cheat."

"Kerry, you are being unreasonable! You want me to beg you, kiss your ass, and cry?"

"No! I want you to be a man and allow yourself to find yourself so the next woman you get you won't lose to stupid shit like this!" I said as I closed the suitcase and lifted it up. He kicked it down, unzipped it, and started to throw my clothes out and onto the floor.

"Drake, what in the hell are you doing? I am not staying, and I'm damn sure not being with you! You can find your whores and have all the fun you want!"

I grabbed the few pieces of clothing he threw, and I placed them back inside my suitcase.

Smack!

Drake hit me across my face so hard I fell to the floor. He then placed his hands around my neck and started choking me. He screamed, "I could kill you right now!"

Then he let me go. I looked up at him holding my face and neck. I gathered myself, caught my breath, and ran out of the house as fast as I could. I got in my car and burned rubber. I headed back to the hospital to see if Cory had made it. I knew then I was going to need some protection just to get my things out of that house.

As I waited in the waiting room area with my hand over my head, I could hear Tony and Cory approaching me. I was nervous about how I looked due to the handprint on the side of my face, along with the red marks around my neck.

"There goes my baby," Cory said as he walked up to embrace me with his hug.

I knew I couldn't just sit there hiding my face, so I stood up to look him directly in his eyes as tears filled my eyes.

"Whoa! What the fuck? Who hit you, KK?" he said before he could even get his arms around me.

"Damn! Whoever it was hit her pretty hard to leave a print like that. Look at her neck, dude!" Tony pointed out.

A loud voice from behind both Cory and Tony yelled, "Don't worry about it, partna!"

My heart skipped beats as the two of them turned to see Drake walking up. My heart was racing in my chest, I was so nervous.

"Say, homeboy, don't walk up on my fam like that!" Tony said as he stepped his foot in front of the two.

"Man, get the fuck out of my way. I came to take my girl back home!" Drake yelled.

"This must be the lowlife that don't know how to treat a woman?" Cory snapped his finger as a thought came back to him. "You're the dude that was with my ex-girlfriend in the hotel pool area. Yeah, they were in the pool trying to fuck in public. Boy, you really fell for the wrong chick. She was setting you up and trying to make me jealous. I saw you two and walked off. She not the saving type, bro," Cory said as he was getting ready for whatever Drake was coming to do. "Now, back up off this one, because I am here to save her, a real woman worth being saved," Cory said as he grabbed Kerry, pulled her close, and kissed her on her lips. He looks up at Drake with a smirk on his face.

Drake balled up his fist and yelled at Cory, "Get your motherfucking hands off my woman, nigga. Kerry, get Yo motherfucking ass over here." Drake paused. "I'm not playing, Kerry," Drake said as the veins in his neck stuck out.

By that time, the hospital nurse had called for security over the intercom.

"Drake, I have nothing more to say to you. Please leave me alone!" I said as I walked backward to corner myself away from him.

Tony noticed what I was doing and walked over to me.

"You don't have to be afraid of him. We not going to let him touch you," Tony said as he stood by me while Cory made sure he was not within reach of me.

"You not about to touch this woman again," Cory said as he stood in Drake's face.

"Man, step back up off me. This shit has nothing to do with you!" Drake yelled as he kept his eyes on me the whole time. I had never seen him act this way before.

"She my woman now, and all that shit you doing stops here and now!" Cory demanded.

"You can stop looking at her like that too, playa!" Tony said, upset by how frightened I looked.

"She is none of your concern now mister, so I suggest you keep it moving before we have a bad misunderstanding, homie!"

Drake walked up to Cory, and Tony held me back, saying, "Let him handle this for you." He walked up to Drake with his fist balled up, and as the two men size each other up, the police came running in. Tony walked over to the officer and gave him the story. He told them he was not on the visitors' list for Michelle and that he needed to be removed as soon as possible. He also said that I might want to press charges for hurting me the way he did.

Cory came to me and kissed me as he caressed my face. Drake was looking at our every move. I could tell this was hurting him. I never put him in these types of situations. I didn't want to see a fight, but I was glad I had a protector on my team.

"He hit me while I was in the process of packing up all my things. He was very upset I was leaving him for good," I told the officer, who walked in behind security. He wrote all this down to make a report. He told me to hang tight while he spoke with Drake.

I walked over to Cory to be by his side. He said, "That is one big-ass coward! No man should hit a woman point blank. He's too damn strong to hit something so soft. I don't care what you have done. There's no excuse to hit you." He pulled me about-face and said, "You won't ever have to worry about me putting my hands on you. You are my queen, and I will show you how much you mean to me."

"My things are still at the house and I want to get them while they still have him in custody," I said.

"Hold on really quick. Let me talk to the police, and we'll see what we can do."

Cory walked over there and told the policeman, right in front of Drake, that I needed to get my things out of the house. He said he was going to accompany me as I packed my things to keep the peace and asked if he would not mind patrolling us to keep the situation safe.

Because I was pressing charges, they were going to take Drake down to the station, so I had time to move my stuff out.

He then walked over to me and said, "Let's go get. Your things."

Now I knew this was not my day, because as we were leaving, Amanda walked up.

"What the fuck is this shit here?" she yelled. Everyone who was in the area stared at us.

"Cory, what are you doing here?"

"I am here with my woman. Now, don't go questioning me about shit," he said with a leer on his face, watching her as she became upset to hear him say "my woman."

"When did she become your woman?"

"When she found you and her old man in the bed together. Just like I found you two by the pool. Thank you for revealing him for the cheater that he is. Now it's my time to show her how a real man treats a woman," he said as he grabbed my hand and we began to walk away.

"Hold up. So, you mean to tell me you two are a thing now, Kerry, after I asked for your forgiveness you do this to me?"

Before I could turn and say anything, Cory addressed. "We have been over for a couple of years now. This sweet woman did nothing to anyone. You and that nigga did this shit on your own. Now, if you would excuse us, we have some packing to do. We will now leave you two with the decision you two have made."

Grabbing my hand and squeezing it tighter, we walked to my car and drove off.

With the extra drama from Amanda, I know it is not the last I am going to hear from her. I know she is upset about me being with her ex-man, but how do she think I felt when I saw her with mine? As I walked out of the house, I left my key on the front room table so that he could see I was never coming back. This felt so good and so right, I knew I should have done this a long time ago. I had no regrets, and I was ready to see what the future held for Cory and me.

As we made our way down the street, I knew this was not finished. I had a funny feeling it was going to get ugly. It was too easy for me to leave. I won't ponder over the possibility, because I know that with Cory, I have a protector in my corner, and as far as Amanda goes, I can handle her.

For now, I am going to live in my positive vibe with Cory, and there isn't a damn thing either one of them can do about it. They wanted to sneak around together. Now they do not have to worry about niggling.

I have my best friend to worry about now. I do not have time for the drama. I hope by the time I make it back to the hospital, Michelle will have opened her eyes. I need to know she will be okay. I know this is less important for me to be telling her, but I know she will be happy to know we have some good men on our team.

Just when I thought the drama was over, we walked back into the hospital waiting room with Amanda still sitting here as if she was waiting on us. Damn it, I spoke too soon.

"Girl, don't you have someplace else to be?" I said.

"You will not get away with having him. He is who I love. I was just using Drake to make you jealous, Cory," she said as she walked closer to Cory.

"Um, you can step back, honey. He is mine now."

"Kerry, you don't have to say a word to her. I pulled out my feelings from her a long time ago," Cory said as he grabbed my hand and we walked off.

"Who do you think you are, and why are you walking away?" she said as if she had any authority to make him stay. "You know I know you better, Cory. When you walk away without finishing something, you go back to it later."

He paused for a second, then turned around walked toward her and said, "Yeah, you are so right. Let me take care of this now so nobody won't have the wrong conception of me." He let go of my hand, got in her face, and said, "I never want to see you again. This is my goodbye, good riddance, and so long lil' momma. I don't ever want to see you let alone be with you ever again." He walked back toward me and grabbed my hand, and as we were walking off, he yelled out, "How is that for a goodbye?"

I must admit, God was looking out for Michelle and me that weekend we found them. We have bagged two good men, and I know we sure as hell are not letting them go. I wish Elle wasn't in the quandary she was in so she could have witnessed the men Cory and Tony had been for me today.

CHAPTER 26

I Will Not Get Caught

Lisa A. Brown

I was in a very eager state of mind to be snooping around in this hospital, dressed up like a janitor, walking from room to room to find this bitch. She must have something I don't to have Tony here with her. He must not know his work associate Carl tells me his every move he makes.

He's a hip white guy who wants to be urban so bad. He used to hit on me back when Tony first started. I used to dodge him—that is, until he told me he wanted to go down on me. Don't get me wrong, I let him fuck, but his head game was on point. All this went down in my husband Tony's office, but that is another story.

Now I must find this bitch and put her out of her misery. As I approached her door, I peeked inside to see if anyone was in there with her. As the coast was clear, I walked in and began to tell her, "You think you can just wave your money around in his face and he'll come falling for you?" I said in an angry voice. "I worked too hard to be with this man, and to think you can just come to him and change his mind?" I said as I walked closer and closer to her stiff body. "You are supposed to be dead, bitch!" I said as I picked up the extra pillow on a chair next to her. I was about to place the pillow over her face. She opened her eyes, and I was caught off guard.

"You are about to die, bitch, and you can't do anything about it," I said as I lifted the pillow back up to her face.

But soon as I was about to suffocate her, a bunch of people just barged in. "Damn," I said as I pretended to cry. "Get well soon." I walked out of the room, making sure no one had a good view of my face.

This bitch has nine lives or something. Hell, the whore would not die. I was the only woman for Tony. If she hadn't shown up, he would have come home to be with me. We were talking about working our problems out.

But no, she had to bring her happy-go-lucky ass to Dallas to make her move on my man. I was happy that Amanda called me giving me a heads-up on this bitch.

As I was leaving the building, I overheard on the news they had a picture of a possible suspect. Stopping to see the evidence they had, I could tell that was my cousin Pat's boyfriend. The news reporter thought he was a woman by how he was dressed. I knew we had played our cards right.

Just to keep myself safe, I might need to leave town and go pay my sister a visit. Hell, her boyfriend likes me and hates our mother and her father. So, I was in the green to go if I needed to. I really didn't know how Pat's boyfriend was going to handle keeping his mouth shut. He could pass for this Michelle bitch in the video. But I know better. They were going to snoop until someone was charged with this crime.

I had to lie low here for a while, because I had to put her down. Eliminate her from the picture and then make my way out of town. I was not going to let this bitch live and point me out for trying to kill her in her hospital bed.

As I was making my way to my car, I noticed Tony and his parents heading inside the building. I had no reason to be here, so I had to leave. Otherwise, they would put two and two together.

"Shit!" I said, mad I didn't get to smother that home-wrecking whore. I had no other choice but to leave town now.

As I made my way, running to gather my things, I knew I had no time to waste. Once someone sees him on TV and figured out it was him, I would be going to jail, because I know he is going to pin it all on me to save his man. So, I gathered all my things and went to the airport to buy me a flight to New Mexico. No one knows me there, and I have enough money to start all over. I kept my cool so I would not be noticed. As I boarded my flight, I asked myself if it was all worth it over a man. I then sat back in my seat as we took off. There was no way I was going down for what my cousin had done. I mean, I know I am responsible too. I just can't go to jail. I'm not built for that place. I hated her for stealing my man, and once this blows over and they find my cousin, then I will come back and try to salvage what's mine.

I hate that she ended up in the hospital and everything, but she needs to know what's mine is mine, and she needs to stay away. I hope they find my cousin before they come looking for me. There was no way I was going down for that ass-whooping he gave her. I just couldn't see myself going down for something I didn't do. Now, after they find him and put his dumb ass in jail, then I will come back home.

The flight was off, and the attendants were making their rounds. I asked for a Crown and Coke to smooth out my nerves. I was glad I was alert to them trying to find me, since my homegirl was one of the cashiers at the car rental place. That was how I knew to get the fuck out of Dodge. I didn't give my cousin a warning because I didn't ask him to beat the bitch to death. That was all him, so he was going to take that charge, not I.

As we were coming to a landing, I gathered myself and my carry-on bags. I made my way out of that airport as soon as I stepped foot on land. I hopped in a cab and told him to take me to the hotel 5 miles from where we were. I paid him for that ride and asked him to stay so he could take me to the nearest Walmart.

I asked him to keep the meter running as I went and shopped for hair dye, makeup, hair clippers, and eyebrow archers. I had to change up my look. I also shopped for food, and I grabbed everything I needed to get to this room.

I worked on changing my hair color to blond with orange streaks. I shaved the side of my head to make my style different. I looked different than before and a whole lot better. I was feeling this new move. All I had to do now was life low until this shit blew over.

I left my old cell phone back at home and bought me a new one. No one could reach me if they wanted to. I had to stay low, and I was going to do so. I can't go down for a crime my stupid-ass cousin committed. I can take the blame for the stolen credit card but an attempted murder charge. That was all on him, and if I had to snitch my way out of it, then hey, I would be one snitching-ass sister. So, until then, Lisa A. Brown is about to lie low, if you know what I mean.

CHAPTER 27

Gathering Information

Detective Vincent Banks and Detective Randy Hall

It was past midnight, and you can say I must have watched that video over a million times to see if I could capture the face of the woman who was covered up in the video. I know she had something to do with this crime; otherwise, why would she be renting a car with the victim's credit card? I made a phone call to my captain to see if he had any insight on where the call was made from.

I was going to crack this case if it was the last thing I did. I asked him to get a judge to issue a warrant for the recorded calls to see if we could trace the number and get a lead in this case. I know this may take a few days since the victim is not dead. The system seems to move faster if it's a murder case rather than an attempt.

Until then, I will be going over this case until I can find other alternatives. That could get me closer to who is responsible for putting her in that hospital.

Two days rolled by and still no warrant. I pressed the issue more and more that this could be the new way a killer can get away and I must put a stop to it. Before I called the captain back,

I put on a pot of coffee. I planned to be up all night working on this case. This was personal since it involved my goddaughter.

Yes, I wanted to help my goddaughter, but the same people might do this again if they got away with it, so I had to put an end to this soon as I found out who was involved.

I called the captain back. He had good news. He gave me the number and address where the card was made. This was all I needed to tie off the loose ends I already had. I called Detective Hall, and we both headed to Texas to the address that was on record from the operator who traced it, along with the voice audio of the operator and the suspect who made the call.

Once I made it back to the office, I sat at my desk thinking of ways to solve this. I called Detective Hall to update him on the visit we needed to pay to the hotel where the call was made from. I told him I had a voice recording and that I had made with the victim a few hours ago. He agreed to the terms of the trip, and we hung up.

I finished writing in the report from the witness who found the door open and the victim lying motionless on the floor. I gathered up all the other things I needed to demand the evidence I had to confiscate so I could put everything in motion to find the suspect and hold them for theft in the stolen credit card and hot checks unit. They would hold her court date off until I could get a for-sure lead.

A sudden knock on my office door and Officer Burnett appeared with the fingerprint scan from the rental car. It had come back clean. I didn't like that result, so I asked her to do another sweep over the entire car. If It was something to be found, we could only find it if it leads us to someone. All we had to do was keep looking and not miss a step.

"I need you to cover every inch of that car."

I had a feeling if I kept my team on their toes, we could find a mistake they had made. I owed it to my deceased friends to find the perps who had done this to my goddaughter. Taking a break, I walked on over to the bar across the street to have a glass of scotch and to hit my cigar. Thinking over it all and backtracking my steps, I called Burnett and asked to re-sweep the house as well. I called my wife to tell her I would not be home.

"Hello."

"Hey, honey. What are you up to?"

"Oh, nothing, my dear. Just finished preparing dinner for us. Is everything all right?"

"Yes and no, darling. I can't seem to get a lead on this case involving Michelle."

"Give it some time, sugar. You will come across something. If there is one thing about a criminal, they leave traces. So just relax your brain, and you will soon think of something."

My wife was always calm and wise when it came to things that seemed unsolvable. She was always the one on my team who could keep my head level. That is why I married her. The love of my life, the reliever of my stress, my rock, and my soft spot.

"I love you, Mrs. Banks."

"I love you too, Mr. Banks. I will bring you dinner, and we can eat together. So, try not to drink too much, baby. You need your mind to be clear to think. I must go. Don't want to burn dinner," she said as she giggled and waited for my response. Then we hung up.

The sweetest thing about being married was being married to a woman like her. She would have made the perfect mother to our children if we could have had some. I was lucky she didn't run off to a man that could have given her children. Still, she chose me, and I am the happiest man alive to be in love with a strong and beautiful woman like Mrs. Banks. She is all mine, and I am all hers.

∼

Reaching the station and heading towards my office, Officer Burnett approached me saying she had a partial print on an open wine bottle. So, I followed her to the lab, and we searched to see if we could pick up a photo of the person the print belonged to. The screen scanned and scanned until it reported no match was found. So, my guess was that this person didn't have a record in the system. So now we know we are dealing with a new criminal.

"Damn it!" I said, slamming my fist on top of the desk.

"Easy, boss," Officer Burnett said as she grabbed her cup of coffee.

"Sorry. I just thought we had a lead, that's all," I replied as I calmed down and placed my hand on my forehead.

"I want to catch this badass too, you know. I have my guys over at Dream's place doing a thorough print sweep as we speak. With Detective Hall and Summers, they will come up with something," she said, trying to lower my stress level.

I could tell she was only trying to help, so I said thanks and walked to my office. I needed to gather myself and just take my time, as my wife suggested.

Pulling out the statement Kerry and the neighbor had written, I reread it over and over to see if I missed something in my search. I was doing everything I could possibly think of to track them down.

Detective Hall called me up and said they had found another print from what looked like her office room closet and another from the jewelry box. He was on his way when he discovered a footprint on the stairs leading from the basement where they had broken in. He gathered up evidence and brought it right to the lab to get a make and size from the shoe print.

Finally, I would get some sort of answer to who this person was. I had to wait until the scans come back with the reports. Until then, I would be in my office, waiting and looking further into what I already had.

I must give it to my team: when we put our heads together, we make it happen. As the day progressed, I traced all that I could possibly traced. There was a knock at my office door, and a tiny voice called out, "Mr. Banks, are you busy?"

"No, baby, come on in," I replied.

"I brought you dinner, and I packed your suitcase, thanks to this nice officer. He helped me bring it all in," my wife said in a sweet and calming voice that made me submit to her entrance.

"Hey there, beautiful," I said as I hugged and kissed her.

"Hi, handsome," she replied, like always.

"Dinner smells very good, baby. What did you cook?"

"Baked chicken and broccoli with Italian seasoning, wild rice, and homemade dinner rolls. I also baked you your favorite cheesecake with blueberries on top."

"Mm, you sure know how to make a man feel special."

"That's what I am here for, morning, noon, and night, handsome," she said, giving me a kiss and then setting up the desk for us to enjoy this meal together. An hour later, Detective Hall and I would be out spending time in Texas to find all the information we needed to get closer to the suspects.

We enjoyed each other's company, and dinner was amazing, like it was every night. I told her I was going to have to take her out once I came back home from this trip. I gazed into her eyes and fell in love just by her smile. When we finished dinner, she walked over to my side of the desk. She began to feed me the cheesecake she had made just for me. Yes, I was so lucky, and I had everything I needed in the woman. She was the best.

Once we were finished, she asked, "So, I heard you went to see Michelle. How is she coming along?"

"The doctor just discovered that her jaw was out of its socket. They braced her face to put it back in place so it can heal."

She squinted her eyes closed. I could see tears forming, so I hurried to change the subject.

"Dinner was delicious, baby. Thank you."

"Vincent Banks do not try to change the subject," she said as she rose up off my lap. I hurried to grab her, sitting her back down.

"No, ma'am, not at all. Just don't want to burden you with the sad news. That is all, honey," I said, deceiving her just a little to protect her feelings. I knew if I told her everything that had happened, she would be stressing herself and Michelle out. Plus, I couldn't have her jeopardizing my job by being on this case.

I hate lying to my wife, and I know this is eating her up because she wants to be there for her. I just told her to sit still and allow me to finish this, and once I put whoever was responsible for this act of crime behind bars, she could visit.

We are her godparents, and we deserve to be there for her, no matter what the circumstances are. I just hope she can see it this way and hang tightly on my word.

As we said goodbye, I walked my wife to her car and opened the door for to get in. We kissed once more and told each other I love you. She drove off, and that is when it hit me.

I needed to call the hotel where the number had been traced, but first I had to see what room number was on the line. That might lead me to all I needed to find this mystery woman. I ran to my desk, looking through the file for the operator number to see if she could search the hotel room number to see if I had a lead on the suspect.

It was going to take some time, but I had a few minutes to waste before I had to head to the airport.

When the operator came back on the line, she told me the number came from the first floor, and the room number could only be known by the hotel manager. I had looked up the special code from the digits the operator had given me. I wrote all this information down and made my way to the airport. I was in luck, and it was all because of my wife. She always had a way of getting my brain to think when she pried into the cases I worked on.

Meeting up with Hall was all I needed to do to board the plane. He had the tickets. When I reached him, I told him about the possible lead I had on the hotel where the credit card company traced the call from. I knew we were in good. All we had to do was get there and find the hotel manager to get him to oblige with the warrant. We boarded the plane, went over the evidence, and had a shot of rum I had in my bag. I had to loosen up before we took off. Flying has never been my thing, and if I did fly, my wife would be holding my hand.

As the plane took off, I was counting down the minutes until we landed. This hour-and-thirty-minute flight was not going to be the cause of me going out of my mind. So, you can say I loved Michelle and my job on this one.

CHAPTER 28

I Never Agreed to Do All That

Chrissy (Pat's boyfriend)

You see, I'm just a transgender woman who acts as a drag queen. Who dresses up for money and prizes? I work for a gay nightclub of exotic dancers. I am a bartender. I only dress up on nights when money is the prize. You see, I travel to different states because I have grown into the competitions. So, when the money is worth traveling for, I go, having full confidence that I will win. Now my man is my bouncer when I put on these drag shows, and he secures the bag for me.

I work hard for a living, and the only bad habit I have is buying and receiving stolen merchandise from my man or people I know that boots. When my honey and his hoodrat-ass cousin came to ask me for a favor, I was willing, if I didn't get caught. I have a lot to lose if I play in criminal situations, so I stand clear of all charges.

I was minding my own business when little missy here came and pulled my man away from me. I told him not to go. You see, Pat and I been together for eleven years, so I know a lot about Lisa that nobody, but family knows. I won't go all into her business, but I know her story. The little drug-selling hooker needs not to cross me or my man while she is missing in action and shit. Pat and I would have never been in this mess she have going on. She came into our life asking for favors. So why wasn't she answering her phone when we called?

We can blame it all on her and she can go down for her own damn crime. Hell, I'm tired of her taking my man and getting him locked up. Then leave me to fix shit up around here. No, ma'am. Not this time. I will rat her ass out.

This is how it all went about. We all had been drinking and playing cards. She asked Pat did he want to hit a lick (that means steal from someone). I kicked Pat leg under the table to get him to say no. He looked at me and asked, when and where? So, I got up from the table and left the house.

I went to the club because I hate when he gets involved with her. He ends up in trouble because he always takes the blame for her, leaving me to bail him out when she turns her back after she gets what she wants. So now you know why I feel some type of way.

Now, do not get me wrong. The money be good. It always pays the bills, and it lasts us a long time. I just want better for my man—you know, like go back to school or get a real job. Don't live your life taking what other people work so hard for.

He just tells me to let him be a man, so I let him. It's just that something didn't feel right to me about this lick. So, I said my peace once I got him alone with me. He hates when I tell him about my bad feelings. But as his girlfriend, honey, I must keep it real (smacks lips), okay?

Not knowing what the job was, I said I want no parts, money, or items. That is when she showed me a picture of the woman she was going to rob. I am light like her, and we both have long, silky, curly hair. So, all I had to do was pick up a rental car from the car rental place. I was game for a fee, all because at that moment, I felt a little jealous of her beauty, and they were just going to take her things. You know, like they weren't going to kill anybody.

Lisa then told me she would hook me up once the job is done. I told her I was going to hold her to it. I went and picked the car up, and once they drove me home, I didn't see them for two days.

Honey had me worried and stressed. I was drinking and calling him 24/7. Once they told me they were on their way back, I was somewhat relieved. Hell, I thought we all was going down. I was worried out of my wits. You don't do that to a transwoman.

So, the next day, I went to work a half a day, because that was the day they were arriving. Once I seen all the goods they were packing, I was all in at whatever they needed me to do. Lisa had a diamond necklace I had to have in my next show. Pat showered me with a lot of brand-new clothes and makeup, famous name-brand everything. He also had flat screen TVs.

I guess I was wrong, because they came back in one piece. But now, I must wonder, who in the hell is she (Michelle Dream) to have all this expensive, classy top-of-the-line kind of stuff? Like, she had it all, and where did she keep it at to have been this easy to take? Honey baby child, she had to have been young and dumb to let these two walks off with such precious things of yours.

All I know is that I received a phone call from one of my cousins telling me I am all over the news. Now I must ask Pat and Lisa what in the hell they got me into. I mean, I was supposed to be an alibi for them. How was I even in the shit to begin with?

As I go on social media to see the video of me getting the rental car, I had no choice but to think they had played me. Now I haven't seen neither one of them since they left me to go sell the goods they stole. I'm no dummy, but I was going to lie low until I knew what to do.

Baby, I tell you, if they think I am going down for a crime they ass obligated, they have another thing coming. So, as I go by my business and continue my living, I know one thing: they will be going down for a crime they committed on their own. Now I must do something different with my hair to make myself look different.

I must hope, wish, and pray that no one turns me in for the reward money. Because once they do, I will be singing like a canary. What did I do to get myself into something big like this? Who was this woman to Lisa for her to be so mean and hateful towards her?

I packed a bag and drove two hours to find Tony to see what in the hell Lisa had done to be on the run.

> Just when you thought things couldn't get any worse …

CHAPTER 29

Out Early Due to Good Behavior

Dewayne

I have been locked up for the past eight years. This last year, I have been permitted by the warden to get out early. I have done all I needed to do to make friends with the warden to get all these good privileges. He has become a good friend and a mentor to me by me being so young when I got locked up on my charges. I worked from the time I arrived all the way until now for him.

Now I have been gone for eight years and some months, but now I ready to see my baby. Michelle, that is. She has always been the girl of my dreams. Funny, I say that to her all the time when we used to be together before I got locked up. She was my baby then and she's still my baby now. I know her parents left her their house.

So, I know where to start when I do look for my baby. I hope she is as happy to see me as I am to see her. She has been in my dreams ever since I been in here. She was the only one I have been with that I took for real. She loves different, she carries herself different, and she respect herself. I need a woman like that.

I have tried to write her a letter stating that I am coming home, hoping she would answer me if I did. But she left me hanging, like all the rest of the letters I sent to her. We used to be inseparable when we were friends. It was even harder for her to let me live once we made love. It was her first time.

I mean, it was mine too—not my first time but the first time I felt something stronger for a woman. I love her, and I always will. We met at school down the seventh-grade hall. She was on her way to class. I stopped her and asked her directions, as if I didn't know where to go.

She was small waisted and long haired, pretty gray eyes and a soft smile, with perfect teeth. She looked up at me, and we locked eyes. I never seen someone so beautiful in all my life. She had me so far gone for real man. But all I know now is that I haven't seen her in eight years, and I am ready. If she is in love, then I'm breaking that shit up.

To be concluded.